# Guardian of

# Eden

# Guardian of Eden

Leslie DuBois

LITTLE
PRINCE
PUBLISHING

Published by Little Prince Publishing in Charleston, South Carolina.
Cover Design: Glendon Haddix

.

ISBN-13: **9780983522003** (Little Prince Publishing)
ISBN-10: **0983522006**

Printed in the United States of America
Visit www.LittlePrincePublishing.com

.

# Prologue:
## Man vs. Evil

"Somebody help, please!"

A man in blue scrubs rushed toward me, took my sister's limp body from my arms and placed her on a gurney. He flashed a light in her eyes and took her pulse as a woman fired questions at me.

"Are you her boyfriend?"

"Boyfriend? She's 12!"

"How long has she been unconscious?"

"She passed out in the car. About 10 minutes. She said her stomach hurts." My voice, usually deeper than most teenage boys', sounded shrill, and broken, almost child-like as it resonated against the cold sterile walls of the near-empty emergency room.

"Is she on drugs?"

"Drugs? She's only 12!" The man and woman wheeled my sister into a room. I tried to follow, but another woman pulled me aside and started examining me, probing me with both her questions and her hands. "What are you doing?" I asked when she lifted up my shirt.

"Where were you stabbed?"

"Stabbed?"

"Yes, I'm trying to find the source of the blood."

"Blood?" I looked down and gasped at the bright-red

stain soaking my shirt and my pants from mid chest all the way to my knees. Trapped in the urgency of the moment, I hadn't noticed the wetness of my clothing. Now that the adrenaline started to wear off, it came into focus. My shirt stuck to my skin where my sister's blood started drying. "Oh my God," I said, allowing my weight to shift towards the wall as I felt my knees weaken. I misjudged the distance and stumbled.

"I think he's going into shock," she yelled, trying to steady me with her gloved hands. "We need another gurney!"

"No, no, I'm fine. Just help Eden, please."

"Are you sure?"

"Yes, the blood's not mine. It's hers."

Her eyes bulged she stepped back and looked at the amount of blood on me. "Dr. Shepherd we need you in number one," she shouted as she whirled away in a blur of white. "The girl's hemorrhaging!" The nurse charged behind the curtain with an IV pole, a bag of fluid, and a fistful of test tubes. I heard her bark orders from behind the ugly blue fabric. "We need stat labs. I think she's going to need refill."

Out of the corner of my eye, I saw Maddie enter the emergency room and run to me. "What did they say? What's wrong with her?" she said. I shrugged and placed my head in my hands. Maddie sat down next to me and rubbed my back. "Don't worry, Garrett. She'll be fine."

I shook my head to fight back the tears. Too many had fallen in my lifetime. At seventeen, I was already tired of crying.

"Garrett, she's strong. She's tougher than you give her credit for. Both of you have had to be to make it this far. You'll make it through this too."Maddie weaved her fingers in mine and lifted my hand to her lips. She tried to comfort me, but her words felt empty and meaningless in my despair. She didn't understand. Yes, Eden and I had been through a

lot of turmoil and survived. I knew how to shield her from all our previous trials. But how do I protect her from what I don't know? She was already sick. Obviously, danger had seeped in and I wasn't there to prevent it. I didn't protect her.

Maddie continued to hold my hand as she started chewing on her bottom lip and tapping her foot. Moments later she let go of my hand, jumped out of her seat then paced the floor while mindlessly snapping her fingers. After about thirty seconds, she sat back down, took my hand, and rested her head on my shoulder as if she might fall asleep. In an instant, she was up again and pacing. Suddenly, she stopped and stared at me.

"We should get you out of those clothes. I'll go see what's in the car," she said as she dashed out of the door to the parking lot. She needed to do something to occupy her time and keep her mind off of Eden.

After she left, I walked up to the reception area and said, "Excuse me, but I brought in the little girl a few minutes ago. Can you tell me anything yet? Is she conscious?"

The short brunette shook her head apologetically. "As soon as I find out something, I'll let you know. You can help things along by filling this out, though." She handed me a clipboard with some papers.

As soon as I sat down, Maddie returned. She handed me a T-shirt. "This was all I could find." She sat down next to me and resumed her nervous habits.

I spent the next fifteen minutes filling out forms. I didn't think to bring Eden's insurance card so I had to recall the information from memory. Usually, I have a perfect photographic memory, but when I'm stressed, it fails. It took several tries before I could see the numbers on her card in my head. I also wrote down everything I knew about Eden's medical history. There wasn't much. Of the two of us, she was always healthier. The only time she had ever been to a

hospital was to visit me. When I finished, I went to the bathroom and cleaned up.

\*\*\*

"Who is responsible for this girl?" The doctor demanded as he stormed into the waiting room.

"I am," I said, standing up so quickly I woke Maddie who had fallen asleep on my shoulder.

"And just who are you?"

"I'm her brother." The doctor raised his left eyebrow and looked me up and down. I knew exactly what he was thinking. "Look, we have the same mother, but my father is black, her father is white. Now can you tell me what's wrong with her?"

"Brother, huh? I think it's time to get the police involved." The doctor turned his back to me and stepped toward the nurse's station.

"Police? What the…?" I reached out and grabbed his shoulder.

I just wanted him to explain, but the doctor reacted to the motion as a sign of aggression and yelled, "Security!"

"Wait, wait, wait," Maddie said, taking my hand and stepping between me and the doctor. "He didn't mean anything. He just really needs to know what's going on. My boyfriend is very protective of his little sister."

The doctor studied the two of us for a few seconds. He must have instantly trusted Maddie's big blue eyes. Everyone did. Including me. She had an innocence, an honesty, in her sweet round face that melted away doubt and suspicion.

"Let me see some identification from both of you." I took out my wallet and handed him my student I.D. while Maddie fumbled around in her purse. She couldn't find her wallet. She dumped the contents of her bag onto the floor and

searched on hands and knees.

"Damn it. I left my wallet," she mumbled as she turned red. Then she whipped off her necklace and stood. "This has my medical information," she told the doctor holding the necklace in front of him. "There's my name and my address and my father's name if you want to call him."

"Bartholomew McPhee?" the doctor asked. "Senator Bartholomew McPhee is your father?" She nodded. He looked from Maddie to me then back. He knew he needed to proceed cautiously in dealing with the daughter of a Virginia senator, especially when that senator currently occupied all the news headlines. He cleared his throat then waved off the security guard. "Do you have any contact information for your mother?" he asked, trying not to seem uneasy about Maddie's parentage.

"She's visiting her mother in North Carolina this weekend." I wrote my mother's cell phone number on his clipboard.

"Eden's in exam room 3," he called over his shoulder as he stormed off to the nurse's station and picked up the phone. Before dialing he added, "If you upset her in anyway, I'm banning you from her room."

Eden started crying and held her arms out to me when I entered her room.

"What's wrong with me, Gary? Am I dying? It hurts so bad." I crawled into bed next to her and held her just like I did when she was little. Cramming ourselves into a small bed didn't bother either one of us. We had slept in worse conditions.

"Shhh. Don't cry. You're not dying. I would never let that happen. The doctors here are going to fix you up and you're gonna be just fine." I stroked her dark blonde hair and stared into her brown-green eyes.

"You promise?"

11

"I promise. I would never let anything bad happen to you." Eden cried harder. She cried herself into exhaustion and fell asleep in my arms.

***

"I brought you some coffee," Maddie whispered as she entered the room. I hadn't even noticed she left.

"You don't have to whisper. She's sound asleep. Eden could sleep through a tornado." I slid out of the hospital bed then took the cup of coffee she held out to me.

"Is she okay?"

I nodded as I took a sip. It tasted wretched. I put the lid back on and placed it on the table.

Maddie hugged herself and stared down at my little sister. She was worried about her. Over the past few months, she'd grown quite attached to Eden. I stepped behind her, put my hands on her shoulders and kissed the top of her platinum blonde head.

"You called me your boyfriend. You've never called me your boyfriend before." Maddie turned around and stared up at me with her blue-lake eyes. Eyes so wide and blue and soft I wanted to drown in them. She stood up straight and wrapped her arms around my neck. She almost couldn't reach even on her tiptoes. At sixteen years old, Maddie was two inches shorter than my twelve-year-old sister. But then again Eden was taller than most twelve-year-olds, a great asset in her modeling career.

Maddie ran her fingers through my long black hair and as tears welled in her eyes she said, "I love you, Garrett."

"I love you, too," I said before pressing my lips to hers. It should have the happiest moment in my life. Madison McPhee loved me. But I couldn't fully enjoy it knowing my sister was suffering just feet away.

12

"What about your father? What about the election?" I asked after kissing her breathless.

"I don't care what he says. I need you, I want you, and I can't exist without you." We both smiled as she repeated the exact same words I'd told her just two weeks ago.

"Now you're just picking on me," I said.

"Well, you have to admit, it's a pretty corny line."

"It wasn't a line. It's the truth." I kissed her again. Our kiss deepened as I pulled her closer to me. I don't know what would have happened if we weren't interrupted by a soft tapping on the door.

"May we speak to you in the hall?" the doctor asked me after poking his head in. "I'm sorry I didn't introduce myself properly," he said once we left the room. "I'm Dr. Shepherd and this is Rowena Smith from Child Services."

I shook both their hands and said, "I don't understand why Child Services is here?" while eyeing them suspiciously. I'd seen enough of Child Services for five lifetimes.

"We spoke to your mother," Dr. Shepherd said ignoring my question. "She faxed over a letter giving you power of attorney over Eden. She trusts you to make all the decisions concerning her welfare." That letter was worthless in my book. I'd already been doing that for the past twelve years.

"Will you tell me what's wrong with my sister, please?" Dr. Shepherd and Rowena Smith exchanged a look, a look of foreboding that instantly made my heart race.

"You might want to sit down, son," the overweight black lady said as she put her hand on my shoulder."

"I don't want to sit down. I want to know what's wrong with her."

Dr. Shepherd sighed and said, "Your sister had a miscarriage." I stared at him blankly as the words swirled around my mind. Everything logical in me told me it was impossible.

13

"I'm sorry. You must be looking at the wrong chart. My sister is only twelve."

"It's not a mistake, Garrett. We've already performed the D&C. The fetus was about 6 weeks old." My knees gave out. I collapsed in a chair. My heart tightened in my chest. My stomach revolted. I thought I might vomit. The doctor kept talking, but I really couldn't hear anything else.

"Who did this? Who could do that to a child?" I asked, interrupting the doctor's details.

"We need your help to figure that out," Rowena said. "Does she have a boyfriend? Is there any chance this was consensual?"

I glared at her. How could she even suggest something like that?

"A detective is on the way," she said once she noticed my fierce expression. "Do you know anything that may help with the investigation?"

I shook my head. I knew nothing. What kind of brother was I to let something like this happen? I should have been paying more attention to her. This was my fault and I was going to fix it.

\*\*\*


Eden began to stir around five o'clock in the morning. I asked Maddie to leave the room for a few minutes. Eden cried for me and I took her hand.

"Eden, I know something bad happened to you," I said as I tucked her hair behind her ear. "I know I let you down."

"Gary, don't cry. It's not your fault." She reached up and wiped a tear from my face.

"Tell me what happened. Tell me who hurt you."
\*\*\*

"Give me your keys," I said to Maddie twenty minutes later.

"Why? Where are you going?" I didn't respond. "Garrett, what's wrong? Is it about Eden?" Her eyes were filled with fear as I towered over her. Maddie handed me her keys and I left the hospital without saying another word.

\*\*\*

I remember picking up the gun and loading it. I even remember pointing it at his head. I remember thinking that I was ruining my life and probably Maddie's as well. I remember the overwhelming need to rid Eden of this evil in her life. What I don't remember is pulling the trigger and pulling it six times.

# Chapter 1:
# In the Beginning

The first time I met my mother, she was eight months pregnant with Eden. I was five and living with my foster mother.

"So how do you feel about meeting your mother?" Mrs. Brooks asked the day of the visit.

"Exuberant," I said as she combed my long jet-black hair.

"That's a big word for a five-year-old. Do you even know what that word means, Garrett?" Mrs. Brooks said.

"Exuberant – adjective. Abounding in vitality; extremely joyful and vigorous." Then I said the word in Spanish and again in French. My foster mother stopped combing my hair and stared at me in shock. She couldn't believe a five year old could have such a vocabulary. Even though I had lived with her for three months, I never spoke much.

I knew a lot of words at that age. Exuberant wasn't even the longest. When I lived with my Grandma Jean, I had to learn a new word every day. She always said that just because we were poor didn't mean we couldn't 'be somebody.' And to her, 'being somebody' started with knowing how to read.

Every morning Grandma Jean took out her old dictionary with the missing pages and picked out a word she thought looked 'pretty.' Then we'd go down to the corner store and she'd ask me to read it to Mr. Jeffries along with the definition. Grandma Jean couldn't read so she wouldn't have known if I pronounced it correctly. I wanted to teach her how to read, but she always said she was too old to learn.

After I used it in a sentence three times with Mr. Jeffries, Grandma and I crossed the street to Mr. Garcia and he'd tell me the word in Spanish. Next, Ms. Claudette at the African hair shop would tell me the word in French.

I could spell and define about a thousand words in three different languages by that age, but I still didn't understand the true meaning of the word "death." It was Mr. Jeffries who knew something was wrong when I showed up at his store one morning without the two most precious things in my life: my grandmother and my dictionary. I lost them both that day. I sat in a squad car for hours while the police and social services searched our apartment for any information about my family. When they couldn't find anything, they sent me to live with Ms. Brooks.

Ms. Brooks thought I wouldn't be there for too long. She just knew my other family wouldn't forget about me. She called me a prodigy and said that she was sure my family was proud of me and would want me back as soon as possible. She was wrong. My other grandmother, my mother's mother, didn't want me because she was white and I was black. My father was incarcerated, so that just left my mother, Holly Jane Whitman and it took her three months to come get me.

"Hi, Garrett. I'm your mommy," Holly said as she knelt in front of me and held her arms out to me. I thought she was beautiful. I finally knew where my green eyes came from.

\*\*\*

17

"What the hell is this?" a bald, white man with tattoos said. I assumed he was my mother's boyfriend and the father of the baby she currently carried.

"I told you I was bringing my son today," Holly said. She held my hand tighter as we entered the motel room she called home.

"That's your son?" He chugged the rest of his beer then said, "I think them foster people made a mistake. That kid is black." He crushed the can on his head then threw it at my mother nearly hitting her in the face. My mother ignored him and showed me to my corner of the room. She had made a pallet of pillows and blankets on the floor. She sat me down and took my Sponge Bob Square Pants backpack off.

I sat on the blankets and stared at an outlet as a roach crawled out of it. I immediately missed Ms. Brooks' house.

I also didn't like the stench of the motel room. Grandma Jean's house always smelled like biscuits and Ms. Brooks house always smelled like finger paints. I didn't know what this place smelled like, but I didn't like it.

"What the hell is the matter with him? Don't he talk?" He got off the bed and came over to me. He looked me over as if I was a dog with fleas that he didn't want in his home.

"Of course, he can talk, Joel. Social Services told me he's really smart. He's reading at a fourth grade level even though he's only in kindergarten," my mother said, stepping in front of the man and blocking his view of me.

"That don't mean nothin'."

"Yes, it does. It means he's a genius." Joel waved his hands in the air and swatted my mother away as if she were some sort of annoying bug. Then he went back to the bed and lit a cigarette. "He's a genius, just like his father," my mother said quietly before turning her attention back to me. "Do you want to lie down for a while, Garrett?" she asked, sitting next to me on the floor. That wasn't easy for her because her

stomach was so big. I nodded. "When you wake up we can go to the store and I'll buy you anything you want. Would you like that?" I nodded. "What do you want to buy?"

"A dictionary."

\*\*\*

By the time Eden was ready to be born, Joel had kicked us out. In his words, he didn't like "smart-ass niggers staring at him all the time." Holly cried for days claiming that she had no one to love her or take care of her. I thought it was for the best. I knew I could take care of her.

I borrowed a newspaper from the school library and searched for places we could afford. Soon we moved to an apartment. It was small, and it still had roaches, but at least it didn't have Joel. Three days later, Eden was born.

Every day I rushed home from school just so I could see Eden and play with her and take care of her. My mother actually depended on me to come home straight from school. By the time I was seven, I was babysitting Eden all by myself. Sometimes my mother would stay out all night and leave me alone with baby Eden. Once, she didn't get back until 1:00 in the afternoon the next day and I had to miss school. I didn't mind though. I was glad I could be there for Eden especially since my mother came home smelling of alcohol all the time.

"Why is that baby crying?" my mother asked one night after she had been asleep all day. Eden had been crying for 20 minutes and it finally woke her up. I was usually really good at keeping Eden quiet while my mother slept. I would read the encyclopedia to her and she'd stare at me with her brown-green eyes like she actually understood me. She was perfectly happy just sitting in my lap for hours on end. But tonight was different.

19

"She's hungry," I said.

"Then feed her." Holly said this as if I hadn't already thought of that.

"There's no food."

"What happened to all those little milks I brought?" She was referring to the little cartons of milk they gave out at school. She, of course, didn't bring them, I did. I would do other kids' homework in exchange for their lunches at school and bring the food home for me and Eden to eat. But since I didn't go to school that day, I had run out of food.

"It's all gone. There's nothing left," I said.

My mother yawned and scratched her head. Eden kept crying.

"Good God, shut up!"

Eden cried louder. My mother stood up and tried to take Eden from my arms.

"Gawie, Gawie," Eden cried as my mother wrenched her away from me. My mother started shaking her. Eden kept crying. Then my mother threw Eden on the bed and slapped her across the face. I lunged for my mother and bit her on the leg. She screamed and fell to the floor.

I felt something warm inside me. It felt like a fire that started in my stomach and went up my chest and up my neck to my face. Everything inside me burned. I stood over my mother and said, "If you ever hit my sister again, I'll kill you." My mother looked scared. She was afraid of her seven-year-old son. There was something in my voice or in my eyes that told her that, if necessary, I *would* kill her.

## Chapter 2:
## The Burning Within

The next morning, my mother was gone. I didn't think anything of it at first. She often left in the middle of the night and met with 'friends.' She usually left a wad of cash on the kitchen table for me and she always returned within a day. I took it as an excuse to skip school and spend some quality time with my baby sister.

With Eden in arms, I checked the kitchen table. No cash. I didn't panic. I figured it just meant she wouldn't be gone too long. I checked the refrigerator and the cabinets. We only had flour, beer, and a can of string beans in the apartment. I took the green beans, cut them into tiny pieces, added water and the flour. Eden ate it up greedily. Either it tasted pretty good or she just trusted me so implicitly, she would eat anything I placed in front of her. Or maybe she was just that hungry. My green bean soup lasted through breakfast and lunch, but by dinner the pot was empty. I read to Eden until she fell asleep. It took longer than usual because she kept pointing toward the refrigerator.

I didn't get much sleep that night in between staring at the doorway waiting for Holly and running to the bedroom to comfort a hungry crying little girl. As the sun rose, so did the tears behind my eyes. What if she never came back? What would Eden and I do? I wondered if Ms. Brooks had room in her home for both of us. What if she didn't have

room and they had to split us up? Suddenly, my throat hurt and I had trouble swallowing. The room starting spinning and I felt weak. I thought I might pass out until I heard Eden crying. She needed me. I had to be strong so I could take care of her. She had no one else.

"Eat, Gawie, Eat," my two-year-old sister said when I entered her room.

I forced a smile on my face and picked her up. "Okay, Bug. We'll eat. But first, why don't you draw me a picture of what you want for breakfast." I spread some paper on the floor and handed her a couple of crayons. I hoped this would distract her long enough for me to think of a plan.

"What do you have there?" I asked when she held up her drawing.

"Cakes!" she said, pointing to the center of the page. That's what she called pancakes.

"What's that?" I pointed to another part of the paper.

"Con-con." That was her word for bacon.

"And I guess those are eggs?" I asked, pointing to a purple scribble. Most of the picture was in purple. It was her favorite color.

She nodded. "Eat now, Gawie? Eat now?"

The dizziness returned along with a churning in my belly. I fought back the tears. I had to be strong.

I loaded Eden into her stroller and started walking. I didn't know where I was going, but I just had to get out of that cramped apartment. I ended up at the grocery store roaming the aisles knowing I didn't have enough money to buy anything. All I had was 75 cents. I fingered the three coins in my pocket as Eden grabbed a box of granola bars from off the shelf.

"Eat?" she asked, holding up the box pleading with her eyes for me to open it.

I silently cursed Holly for doing this to her. I could

understand why she would leave me. No one besides Grandma Jean had ever wanted me. But how could she leave such a sweet, innocent, beautiful little girl?

My anxiety turned to anger as I did something I never thought I'd do. I pushed Eden's stroller into the bathroom with the box of granola bars. We sat in a stall and ate the whole box. Eden laughed and giggled as she smeared chocolate on her face. My anger subsided as I watched the joy on her angelic face.

I filled the empty container with a roll of toilet paper then placed it back on the shelf. On the way out, I bought a can of milk so it wouldn't seem like I had been wandering around the store for no reason. I felt guilty stealing food, but I had no choice. I had to feed my baby sister.

I didn't want to have to steal again, so before we got home, I stopped at Wendy's and stuffed my pockets full of condiments and crackers. That night, I made tomato soup with the ketchup packets, canned milk, and water.

Two days later, as I came home from another 'shopping' expedition, I found my mother in the kitchen.

"You two must be hungry. I made grilled cheese." My mother placed two plates on the table and gestured for us to sit down. Eden ran to our mother and wrapped her arms around her legs completely forgetting and forgiving the fact that she had abandoned us for four days.

"Where were you?" I asked. My mother ignored my question as she picked up Eden, placed her in a chair and handed her an entire grilled cheese sandwich. "That's too big for her. You have to break it up." I grabbed the sandwich out of Eden's hand and tore it into little pieces.

"She's fine, Garrett. She has teeth, you know. You worry too much."

"Well, someone has to worry about her. You obviously don't." I folded up the stroller and threw it behind

23

the couch.

My mother closed her eyes and sighed. "I guess I deserve that."

"Well, where have you been?"

"Look, baby, I got into some really bad stuff and I was really messed up and I didn't want you to see me like that. I came back as soon as I got cleaned up. Didn't Sharlinda from next door look in on you?" I shook my head. "I'm so sorry, Garrett. It won't happen again."

I stared at my mother and tried to believe her. I couldn't. She smiled at me and held out the sandwich as a peace offering. I shook my head and went to my room. She disappeared like that two more times that year alone.

***

"I said not tonight, Jimmy!" I heard my mother's voice through the paper-thin walls of our little apartment. It was three o'clock in the morning but I wasn't asleep. I never slept much. Not at home anyway. I had to be alert to protect my mother and Eden.

Four-year-old Eden was curled up in a ball next to me in the bed we shared. She could sleep through anything, but not me. I always knew when my mother was fighting with one of her boyfriends. I moved Eden aside as I crawled out of bed. I opened the top drawer of my dresser, the drawer Eden couldn't reach, and pulled out the knife I hid there.

I called 911 then went to my mother's room. Jimmy was on top of her. Holly was crying and trying to twist out of his grasp. He had her arms pinned above her head with one hand and was ripping off her clothes with the other. I remember he was naked and sweaty. I knew he needed to be stopped.

"Jimmy, you're drunk! Stop it! You're gonna wake my

kids!"

"If you just shut up and give me some, they won't wake up!"

"She said no!" I yelled with my hands behind my back concealing the knife.

"Garrett sweetie, go back to bed. I can handle this." My mother tried to sound calm, but I could see the terror in her face.

Jimmy looked at me and laughed. I showed him the knife to make him stop laughing, but he didn't. Anger ignited a fire in me and I lunged for him. Jimmy's eyes widened with surprise at my strength. Pain and fear flashed in his eyes as I plunged the knife into his leg. Jimmy screamed in agony. My mother screamed in horror.

"You damned little nigger!" he yelled, reaching behind to grab my neck. He squeezed tighter and tighter until it was hard for me to breathe. My mother picked up a lamp and hit Jimmy over the head with it but he didn't loosen his grip. Suddenly, I felt like I was flying, then everything went black.

\*\*\*

"Are you gonna die, Gary?" Eden asked as she crawled into my hospital bed with me. Jimmy had thrown me against the wall giving me a concussion and breaking my arm. I didn't regret stabbing him. He deserved it. And I didn't even care that I had gotten hurt in the process. I was just sorry that Eden had to see me in pain.

"No, I'm not going to die." I hugged her tightly even though my arm was killing me.

"Cause if you died, who would take care of me?" My mother stood in the doorway. She started crying when she heard Eden's question. Her beautiful face had been beaten black and blue. I felt sorry for my mother as well. For all her

faults, she didn't deserve the treatment she received from men. I wondered how she ended up that way. What had gone so wrong in her life to cause her to make one bad decision after another and cling to men that did nothing but hurt her? How did she end up with no one to protect her? No one, except me.

"Garrett, baby, I'm so sorry. I'm gonna be a better mother. I promise." My mother hugged me and Eden, but I didn't really feel like hugging her back. "Don't you believe me? I'm gonna take care of you. I am. Don't you know I love you?" She pleaded. I stared into her green eyes. The eyes that were exactly like mine. I tried to believe her. I wanted to believe her, but I just couldn't.

***

After the incident with Jimmy, Eden and I went to live with Ms. Brooks for a while. My social worker forced me to see Richard every week instead of every month. Richard Fielding was my psychologist. He was supposed to rehabilitate me even though there was nothing wrong with me.

"So you don't see how attacking a man three times your size is dangerous?" he asked while cleaning his glasses with a tissue.

"Of course, I see the danger in it. I'm not an idiot. But I had to do it. He was hurting my mother. Holly can't take care of herself sometimes."

"Don't you know he could have killed you?"

"That's why I had the knife." I was quickly tiring of Richard's stupid questions.

"But he's bigger and stronger than you."

"Well, maybe next time, I'll need to use a gun instead." Richard sighed and rubbed his temple. I think I was giving him a headache. I frustrated him. He would never be able to convince me that it wasn't my duty to protect my family.

"Holly tells me you're still having headaches and throwing up at night. Is that true, Garrett?" Richard asked, trying to change the subject somewhat. I shrugged. I didn't like to consider myself sickly, but since I had started living with Holly, I did suffer from headaches and stomach aches a lot. And now, on top of that, I also had nightmares. On the rare occasions that I could actually sleep, I dreamt of monsters coming to attack my family. Some nights I ended up in the bathroom vomiting for hours.

Richard thought I had some sort of nervous disorder due to the stress of my home life. I tried not to talk about it with him too much. I didn't want him to take me away from Eden and Holly to put me in some sort of hospital for evaluation.

"Garrett, I would like an answer," he said when I hadn't provided any additional information along with the shrug.

"I'm fine. My head's fine, my stomach's fine, I'm fine." I folded my arms and waited for his next question, but I think he'd given up.

"We're done for the day, Garrett. Why don't you go play in the waiting room?" Richard ushered me out of the door and signaled for Holly to enter. Eden was in the waiting room engrossed with the dolls they provided. She smiled at me hoping I would go play with her. I didn't feel like playing dolls. Even at that age I realized my role in the family. I was the man of the house. Men didn't play with dolls. Instead, I sat by Richard's door and listened to what he told Holly.

"I'm really concerned about his temper," Richard was saying. "He's nine years old and he's getting into knife fights. This violent streak is going to land him in jail or worse."

"It's not a temper. He doesn't have a violent streak. He

just wants to protect me. Just like his father. He's gonna end up just like his father. I can't go through that again."

*** 

When Eden and I went back to live with my mother, my social worker went through the house and removed all knives and sharp objects. We didn't even have pens or pencils in the house, only crayons and markers. It was ridiculous. As if I didn't know where to find a knife if I needed one. And I really did need one when Joel came back.

## Chapter 3:
## Let There Be Light

My mother had a textbook case of low self-esteem. I read about it once while I waited for Eden to finish her appointment with Richard. That was the only explanation I could come up with for why she would let Joel back into her life.

When I was about 11 years old, we lived in an apartment on Sunny Lane in Oxon Hill, Maryland. Life was anything but sunny, however. The constant sound of police sirens or girlfriends yelling at unfaithful boyfriends in the middle of the night didn't bother me too much. I could even live with the scratching sounds that came from inside the walls and the ceiling which I hoped were mice but I knew were rats. We had lived in worse places. What *did* bother me was Joel. I never got any sleep with Joel in our home. I didn't trust him. I lay awake in bed at night listening and waiting for him to do something violent just like Jimmy did.

I remember there used to be a man with a saxophone that played on the street corner late at night. He would open his case and let people throw in money. I never had any money, but I did like to add words to the sounds that drifted up to our apartment.

*Black is dark and dark is night*

29

*A welcome dark for rest and respite*
*Where dreams are made to fill the empty road of life*
*A trail traveled alone with no end in sight*
*Or maybe the end is near and I haven't got it right*
*Maybe death isn't as hard as this empty life*

"What the hell are you writin' over there?" Joel slurred. He sat on the couch drinking beer and smoking. I'd found a place in the corner of the living room and scrawled my nonsensical saxophone lyrics. "Are you writin' somethin' about me? You better not be writin' about me, boy."

I ignored him and continued writing. Maybe the lyrics weren't nonsensical. Maybe they revealed what I really felt. Not to say I wanted to kill myself or anything. I just felt more at ease, less anxious inside by getting these words out on paper. Maybe I would make this kind of writing a regular habit.

I looked over at my almost six-year-old baby sister sleeping on the couch next to Joel. How could she stand to be so near to him? I knew he was her father, but he treated her just as bad as he did Holly. He never hit them or anything, not in front of me anyway, but he constantly insulted them and brought them to tears. Still, both Holly and Eden flocked to him as if they needed him.

I put my pencil down and continued to stare at my sister curled up on the couch in a tight little ball. She was so beautiful I smiled to myself. I did everything in my power to take care of her and make her happy, but I wasn't enough. She still needed the love and attention of a father.

Suddenly Joel screamed, "Are you laughing at me?" I shook my head no, but he didn't believe me. What happened next, I'd rather not talk about. Not yet anyway.

That same year, Eden lost her two front teeth. I assured her this was normal and that they would come back, but she was convinced she was a hideous monster. She refused to look at herself in the mirror and cried pitiful tears if she got an accidental glance.

"I'm so ugly. That's why nobody wants me," she cried one day after brushing her remaining teeth in the mirror.

"What do you mean? Who doesn't want you?"

"My father doesn't want me. Is that why he left again? Because I'm ugly?"

"No, Eden, of course not. He left because…" I wanted to say he left because he was a disgusting cretin that didn't deserve to live with us in the first place, but I wanted to respect the fact that he was her father. "He left because he and Holly didn't get along anymore. It had nothing to do with you."

"Does mommy love you more than me because you're more beautiful? Why can't I be pretty too?"

"Mommy doesn't love me more than you. She loves us the same." I had no idea where Eden would come up with such an idea.

"She does, she does. You should hear how she talks about you to other people. She brags about how smart you are and how you help around the house so much and how she doesn't know if she'd be able to make it without you in her life. She never says anything like that about me."

I learned to be very careful when talking with Eden about beauty and self-image. I didn't want her to grow up and have the same problems our mother did. Every chance I could I tried to convince her how beautiful she was. It completely confused me how she could think otherwise.

After watching my mother struggle through relationships, I vowed that I would never do the same. Not only would I never treat a woman the way Holly's boyfriends treated her, but I would make sure that I was only with

someone that loved me as much as I loved them. And I wanted to make sure Eden grew up with a confidence that demanded respect from the opposite sex. She needed to know she deserved the best.

Holly tried to be a better mother. She did the best she could. After Joel tired of being a parent, he moved out and our lives began to improve. She stayed away from men completely for about six months. I think it was part of one of her rehab programs.

We moved to a better neighborhood and Holly got a real job as a secretary at a beauty salon. They did her hair and make up for free sometimes and made her even more beautiful than she was naturally, thus, enhancing her attractiveness to men. Men were more of a weakness for her than drugs or alcohol and she slowly slipped into old habits. As the years went by, I didn't like strange men being around my little sister all the time.

"Garrett, I swear, you're gonna give yourself an ulcer one day," my mother said blithely after I'd expressed my concerns to her. I was fifteen and worried about the attention my ten-year-old sister started to attract from the opposite sex. Eden was 5'5" with waist-long dark blond hair, perfect fairy like features and an angelic smile. One of my friends even commented on how gorgeous she was and how she didn't look ten years old. After the broken nose I gave him healed, though, he never said anything else about her.

"I'm serious, Holly. I don't want all these random men hanging around the house anymore. It's not safe. What if one of them tries something with Eden?"

My mother continued trimming some flowers over the kitchen sink as she said, "Really, Garrett, do you have to call me Holly? What about ma or mom? I'll even go with mother."

I'd tried to call her mother for a while. It didn't work.

Besides the fact that it just didn't feel natural to me, I got tired of the strange looks from people when we were in public. She looked too young, I looked too old. She was white, and I was not. It was just too much to explain. I'm sure people just assumed we were boyfriend and girlfriend sometimes.

I sighed and said, "I would like to meet the men before you bring them into the house. Before they meet Eden. Can we just be in concurrence about the matter?"

"Concurrence? Is that the word of the day?" she teased. I ran my fingers through my shoulder length hair. She could be so frustrating sometimes. "Is that how you talk to the girls your age? No wonder you don't have a girlfriend. And you should have a girlfriend. You're such a handsome young man." She turned to me, looked into my eyes and caressed my cheek. "Beautiful green eyes, strong masculine jaw, broad shoulders. I swear to God, it's like you just went shopping for genes and picked out the best features between me and your dad." She went back to trimming her flowers. I paused and stared at the back of her golden hair. She'd never mentioned my father to me before.

For some reason, he was a taboo topic. I wanted to ask her to go on, but I figured she would clam up and end the conversation like always. Fortunately, she seemed ready to talk without any prodding. She took a vase out of the cabinet under the sink and filled it with water as she said, "He was the sexiest man I'd ever seen in my life. He was 6'5", muscles everywhere, dark chocolate skin, and a smile that made me weak in the knees. We were only sixteen when we had you." My mother took the vase, put the flowers in it then walked toward the living room.

"Did you love him?" I asked, following her. She nodded.

"I still do," she said wistfully as she stared at nothing.

"Why did he go to jail? What did he do?"

"Gary, I need help with my homework," Eden called from her bedroom.

"Garrett, help your sister, then get changed for dinner," my mother said, snapping out of her reverie and nervously wiping her hands on her skirt. She tried to sound authoritative and motherly. She didn't have to tell me to help my sister. I always did it anyway. "We're having a visitor for dinner." She smiled and bounced into the kitchen. It was like she just flipped a switch and reverted back to her carefree demeanor without a second thought about my father or the conversation we were just having.

"Hol…Mother! What did we just talk about?" I followed her back into the kitchen. "You can't just bring some guy into our home."

"He's not just some guy. He's *the* guy. I really like this one. He's different, I swear," she exclaimed clasping her hands like an infatuated teenager. "I met him at the salon. He's a photographer. He has his own studio and everything. And best of all, he treats me real good."

"Well," I corrected her.

"Well, what?"

"He treats you well not…oh never mind." I wanted to scream and punch the wall, but I had to control my temper. Richard and my social worker were still concerned about my anger level. I took a deep breath then went to help Eden with her homework.

\*\*\*

"So, do you like this one?" Richard asked in reference to my mother's new boyfriend, Corbin. Before I could even answer he took the cap off of his pen and started writing. I hated when he did that. It made me feel like my answer

34

didn't matter.

"He's okay." I shifted uncomfortably in the miniscule chair. All of the furniture in his office was too small. He was a child psychologist and I was no longer a child. I was fifteen and over six feet tall, but my social worker still wanted me to see him every month.

Richard stopped writing and looked up from his notepad. "Did you say 'he's okay'?"

"Yeah, why?"

"You've never described one of your mother's boyfriends as 'okay'." I shrugged as Richard began flipping through his notes. "According to my records, Tom was insipid, Brian was asinine, Larry was intolerable, Jimmy was virulent. I don't even know what that means."

"Virulent - adjective. Intensely bitter, spiteful or malicious."

"Buster was inadequately compensating for his intellectual and physical deficiencies," Richard continued reading from his notes and ignored my interjection. "And Joel was the Devil incarnate." He looked up and waited for me to respond. When I didn't he said, "You must really like this guy."

"He's okay," I repeated while folding my arms over my chest. Honestly, he was more than okay. He was wonderful. My mother was right. He *was* different. That first night he came for dinner, he not only brought my mother flowers, but he brought Eden a doll and brought me an exquisite antique thesaurus. No man had ever brought my mother flowers let alone gifts for me and Eden. I'd tried for six months to find fault with him and I couldn't. He was like a light that had entered our dark lives.

"Well, according to Eden, he's the best thing to ever happen to your family." I didn't say anything, but Richard started scribbling furiously.

"What are you writing?" I yelled.

"Do you really want to know?"

"No, I don't want to know. I'm just asking because I enjoy the docile tone of my own voice." Richard rolled his eyes at my sarcasm and unbuttoned the top button of his shirt. Large wet circles were forming under his armpits. Even though I'd known him for over ten years, I think he was afraid of me. I think my intelligence made him nervous.

"Simply stated, I think you have a Superman complex." Here we go again. Richard tried to relate everything to comic books. I think it came from him being a child psychologist for too long. "You're not happy unless you're rescuing someone. You need to be needed. If you're saving your mother or Eden, you know where you belong, you know what to do. Now that Corbin has come along and proven to be a good guy, there's no one for you to save. And you don't know what to do." Richard sat back and waited for my smart aleck retort, but I couldn't think of anything to say. He was so shocked by my silence, his formidable ass nearly fell out of the chair.

What if he was right? Up until that point, the events in my life had fashioned me into the hero of the family. I made sure food was in the house. I made sure Eden went to school every day and that Holly got up for work. I was the one that chased away old boyfriends at knife point in the middle of the night or threw away my mother's drugs or alcohol in order to keep her sober. Now there was Corbin.

***

"I wrote you a poem," Eden said to Corbin one night while we were having dinner. I'd infused my love of words into Eden and she slowly developed into a talented poetess. She stood up from the table and took a sheet of pink paper out of her pocket. She cleared her throat and read:

*With the flash of a camera*
*A new picture has begun*
*The dark clouds have parted*
*Here comes the sun*
*No need for fear as our plight has ended*
*Our hope has come*
*A new family transcended*
*Let there be joy*
*Let there be light*
*Let there be emotion*
*With no more fright*
*Let there be peace*
*Let there be light*
*Let our mistaken path*
*Become right*

Corbin cried and a week later, he proposed to my mother.

Now that we were safe and happy, I guess, in a way I felt less relevant. I felt like less of a man. That was until I met Maddie.

# Chapter 4:
## Swallowed Soul

I'll never forget the feeling I had the first time I took in her enchanting blue eyes. My heart pounded in my throat. I leaned against my locker to portray an air of aloofness when in reality I needed a solid object for support. Immediately the words for my next poem came to mind. I didn't write poetry too often, only when I was truly inspired.

"You must be Garrett Anthony," she said.

"No…,"

"You're not?" Her eyes widened with disappointment. She really wanted me to be Garrett Anthony. Looking at her little round face, I wanted to be anything she wanted me to be. Then, suddenly, I remembered, I *was* Garrett Anthony. I had to get used to going by Corbin's last name. The adoption wasn't final. He still had to get Eden's father and my father to sign away their parental rights. Both men were making the situation difficult.

After the wedding, Corbin decided to send us both to Barton Arms Preparatory School. I didn't want to go. I didn't like the idea of wearing a uniform everyday or riding the metro for forty-five minutes into D.C. each morning and afternoon. I also didn't think I'd fit in at this school. I'm surprised they even accepted me given my "propensity for violent outbursts" as Richard put it, but they did. The only reason I agreed to go was because it meant Eden and I could go to the same school. I think deep down I liked the idea of getting such a good education from such a reputable school, but I just didn't feel like I deserved it or that it would last.

"I mean, yes, I am Garrett Anthony. I'm just not used to the name, yet." She smiled broadly and stared up into my eyes. I waited for her to keep talking and explain how she knew my name, but she didn't. She just smiled and stared at me. I didn't mind really. I enjoyed looking at her. I could've stared into her eyes all day.

"Oh! I'm sorry," she said finally. "I'm staring. I don't mean to stare. I'm doing an article for you about the newspaper." I raised an eyebrow in confusion and relaxed in the knowledge that she was just as nervous and had a harder time hiding it. "No, I mean," she giggled. "I'm doing an article *about* you *for* the newspaper."

"Me? Why are you writing an article about me?"

Her mouth flew open. I could read the shock and bewilderment in her eyes. They overflowed with honesty and expression betraying any emotion she could possibly feel.

"Are you kidding me?" She swallowed hard and licked her lips. My God, she had beautiful lips. They were so full and red and just plain succulent. I didn't even know the girl's name and I wanted to kiss her. I wanted to kiss her so badly my chest began to ache. "You earned a perfect score on the SATs and you took them in the ninth grade! You finished the entrance exam to get into this school in record time. I heard that the admissions department wanted you to come here so badly that they didn't even ask you to cut your hair."

I touched my ponytail as I inspected the students passing by. They looked like white clean-cut robots - an army of future Ivy-leaguers preparing to start their today in preparation for bright, powerful tomorrows. I really didn't fit in. How did I end up going from foster homes and psychologists to Barton Arms Preparatory School? It was a

tenuous dream wrought upon a bubble of uncertainty. And I knew the bubble would soon burst.

"You're not going to print that are you?" The last thing I needed was for them to change their mind and decide to make me cut my hair.

"Don't worry. It won't matter. No one reads my articles anyway."

"I'd read them." The beautiful blue-eyed creature turned red and stared at her shoes while adjusting her overloaded backpack. I think I embarrassed her.

"Well, anyway," she said as the first bell rang, "Can I interview you for my story?"

"Yeah sure. Of course."

"Okay, great."

"Okay."

"It was nice to meet you, Garrett," she said as she backed away while still embracing me with her eyes. Suddenly, she stopped short and ran back to me, her blond curls bouncing all the way. "I'm Madison, like the president. Not the current president, like the fourth president of this country, but, of course, you would know that since you're a genius." She blushed again and looked down at her shoes. "Um, anyway, everyone calls me Maddie."

\*\*\*

Over the years, I'd discovered something about myself. Inside, I felt angry, unsure, and alone. These feelings manifested in one of three illogical ways. Either I found some unsuspecting victim and took out my frustration on his face, I locked myself in the bathroom and puked until I was empty inside, or I wrote a poem then set it on fire so no one would ever see it. After meeting Maddie, I settled on option number three.

*I had never seen a blue*
*so deep*
*so wide*
*so all consuming*
*Eyes that seize*
*my air*
*my thoughts*
*Eyes that entomb me*
*With one look I died*
*a sweet death*
*from the passion that*
*overwhelmed my soul*
*Her eyes had*
*captured my spirit*
*and swallowed me*
*whole*

"Who's Maddie?" Eden asked as we rode the metro home after school.

"Just a girl."

"What's so special about her? Why are you writing a poem about her? Why do you have her name written all over your notebook? I thought only girls did that."

"She's just a girl from school," I responded, covering my notebook with my Latin book.

"Oh, come on, Gary. You can tell me the truth. We tell each other everything. I told you when I was in love with Brendan."

"You were eight. And you got over it when you found out he still wet the bed."

"So, I still told you." Eden crossed her arms and sulked in her seat. I felt a little guilty about excluding her. She was right, we did tell each other everything, but this was

41

different.

"Look, Eden-bug, I just met her. I don't know how I feel about her. But when I figure it out, you'll be the first to know, all right?" Eden smiled that smile that melted my heart. The smile that I'd seen every day for the past 11-and-a-half years. I swear, she smiled that smile at me the day she was born.

Eden hopped out of her seat on the train and started dancing around chanting, "Gary's in love, Gary's in love." It was a ridiculous showing, but Eden's beauty allowed people to ignore her silliness. They were mesmerized by her. A few people even clapped. Eden had a different way of dealing with her inner demons. She became somewhat of a theatrical genius. Sometimes even I had a hard time reading her true emotions and I knew her better than anyone in the world. The shy six-year-old who once thought she was too ugly to look at herself in the mirror now loved to dress up and prance around the house as if she walked a runway in Europe. I guess it was a girl thing.

Eden took a bow, basking in the attention, before returning to her seat next to me.

"I hope you're finished," I said, pretending to be upset with her.

"For now." She smiled slyly as I tousled her long dark blonde hair.

"You want to play our game to pass the time?" I asked.

She nodded excitedly.

"Okay, we're on the letter H, right?" I said, just trying to make sure she'd been paying attention.

"Unh-uh, we're on I. We did H last Wednesday on our way home from the library," she said shaking her head.

"Right, right. Okay, minimum length is six letters. I'll start with…indolent."

"Iconic."

"Impasse."

"Information," she said with a sly grin.

"Oh come on, Eden. That's cheap."

"What? It's more than six letters," she responded innocently.

"You know the rules. You have to use words not common in everyday language. Sophisticated words."

"Okay, okay. What about…indigenous?"

"That's my girl."

***

"Why don't you tell me about that fight you were in when you lived with Ms. Brooks?" Richard asked me this question about three times a year since it happened when I was nine-years-old. You would think by now I would have a suitable answer, but I didn't.

When Eden and I went to live with Ms. Brooks after my fight with Jimmy, there was this kid named Elias Castillo. He was two years older than me but he looked my size maybe smaller. Elias stuttered, twitched uncontrollably and sometimes wet his pants at the slightest provocation. All of his problems came from the fact that his mother used drugs when she was pregnant with him. The other kids would taunt him by asking him a simple question. When the slow stuttering response came, they would laugh and call him 'crack baby' which would trigger the twitching and the pants wetting. It was a vicious cycle. One day I got tired of it.

"Hey, Elias, what day is it?" twelve-year-old DeMarcus asked, stepping in front of the television where Eli had been watching cartoons.

Immediately his partner in crime, Terence, started laughing and said, "By the time he answers it'll be tomorrow.

"I asked you a question, retard. Now what day is it?"

"Tu…Tu…Tu…," was all that came from Eli.

I tried to ignore the scene at first. I sat in the corner and concentrated on the hand-held electronic Scrabble game that Mr. Jeffries had sent me in the mail. But when DeMarcus pushed him down, I decided I had to do something.

"Does terrorizing an innocent make you feel particularly stalwart?" I asked still sitting in my corner of the living room. Stalwart was my word for that day. I had found it in the newspaper then asked my teacher what it meant when I went to school.

"What the hell are you talking about?" DeMarcus probably didn't understand a single syllable I'd said.

"I'll say it again, but this time slowly and with smaller words." I stood up and approached the bully. He was a good three inches taller than me, but for some reason I wasn't afraid. Maybe I should have been. "Beating up on people who can't defend themselves only makes you look stupid."

DeMarcus stared at me utterly surprised that I would call him stupid to his face. He opened his mouth to say something then closed it again. I could see his jaw tightening in anger. Then, without another word, he punched me in the face so hard I fell backwards right on top of where Eli had just wet himself. Even though the room was spinning, I still managed to see DeMarcus and Terence laughing. Then I heard him say, "Who looks stupid now?"

What happened next is a little hazy. All I remember is sitting in my room holding my cracked electronic Scrabble game. Eli told me later that I tackled DeMarcus and bashed his head in with my game.

Seven years later, I still didn't remember what I did to DeMarcus. What did that mean?

"What does that mean?" I asked Richard when I'd finished recounting as much as I could.

Richard stopped writing and looked at me. I think it surprised him that I actually asked him a question as if I wanted to engage him in conversation. Our sessions usually consisted of him asking all the questions and me giving as many one word responses as possible.

"Um, I don't know."

"How can I send a boy to the hospital to get seven stitches in his head and not remember? What's wrong with me?"

Richard cleared his throat, cleaned his glasses, then said, "I think you've had an extremely difficult life and you don't quite know how to deal with your emotions. You're angry over the hardships you and Eden have suffered and rightfully so, but you have to learn an appropriate release for that anger or else it will consume you."

His psycho babble didn't answer my question. What did anger have to do with memory lapse? I could only take solace in the fact that it hadn't happened again since. Or, if it did, I didn't remember.

\*\*\*

"Get dressed," my mother said to me one Saturday morning as I read the newspaper. It was seven o'clock in the morning. A full three hours before my mother usually awakened.

"Why? Where are we going?"

"I'll explain in the car. Just put on something nice. Do you still have that suit you wore for your eighth grade graduation?"

"Holly, that was three years ago. It won't fit me."

"Well, borrow a shirt and tie from Corbin." I stared at

45

my mother trying to read her emotions. Her eyes were red and puffy with the obvious remnants of tears.

"Holly, what's wrong? Did Corbin hurt you?" I sat upright in my chair.

"No, of course not." She sighed. "This is not about me. Not exactly, anyway. It's about you. Now get dressed. We have a long drive."

"Did I do something wrong? Are you sending me back to foster care? What about Eden? Is she coming too?" I stood up from the table in a panic.

"Oh, my poor baby," she said embracing me. "No, it's nothing like that." She pulled away from me and wiped tears away from her face with the back of her hand. "We're going to see your father."

## Chapter 5:
## Sins of the Father

"My father? What…why…where…" I took a step back and stared into my mother's tear swollen eyes.

"I'll explain in the car, Garrett," she said turning away so I couldn't read her emotions.

"What about Eden? I promised to take her to the Air and Space Museum today."

"She's gonna go on a photo shoot with Corbin instead."

"But…but…" I had studied countless words and phrases. I'd studied Latin, Greek and French to become more acquainted with word origins and the true complexities of language. My word obsession proved fruitless in this instance. For no words could describe what I felt. I made a mental note to create a poem about it later.

Even though my mother promised to explain along the way, we drove in silence. I think there were things she wanted to tell me, but she didn't know how. Several times she inhaled sharply like she wanted to start a sentence. Then seconds later she'd exhale and shake her head.

The deafening silence slowly drove me insane. Questions bounced around my mind with spasmodic frequency. What would he look like? Why did he go to jail? Why hadn't I ever met him? Why after so many years of never even mentioning his name did my mother suddenly want to take me to him? All these questions might soon be

answered when I met my father for the first time.

"We're leaving Virginia?" I asked, as we passed the state line. It was the first time either of us had said a word in almost two hours.

"Your dad's in a prison in North Carolina." I hoped she would continue, but she didn't. The silence returned and allowed my mind to wander back to the unanswered questions that engulfed my life.

When we reached the institution, my mother turned off the engine, gripped the steering wheel with both hands, and stared straight ahead.

"I can't do this. I can't see him." She turned to me and said, "You're gonna have to go alone."

"Alone?" I asked terrified. I wasn't afraid of the prison. I'd been inside one before. In the sixth grade, after I'd been suspended for fighting for the fifth time, my social worker took me to a jail in Arlington to try to scare me straight. I remember thinking that I'd slept in much worse places than the Arlington County Jail.

No, prisons, prison life, not even prisoners scared me. What terrified me was the prospect of meeting my biological father. For some reason, even though I'd never met the man before, I felt as though I needed his approval. What would I be if I didn't get it?

"Holly, I'm under eighteen. I seriously doubt they'll let me in there alone," I said, hoping the statement was true.

"Well, I'll get you in there, but you have to visit him by yourself. I mean, I haven't seen him since I married Corbin." My mother pulled out her makeup bag and began to reapply her lipstick. I stared at her dumbfounded.

"You married Corbin three months ago. You saw my father three months ago?" My mother closed her eyes tightly and clasped the bridge of her nose with her thumb and forefinger.

"I can't talk about this right now, Garrett. Let's just go and get this over with." My mother opened her door.

"No!" I grabbed her wrist and pulled her toward me. "I want to know why you saw my father three months ago but I don't even know his name."

My mother's eyes bulged as she said, "Garrett, calm down, okay. Let me go, baby, please." I saw fear in my mother's eyes. I looked down and saw how violently I clutched her wrist. Shame stifled the anger that had erupted in me and I instantly let her go.

"I'm sorry mother." I slouched in my seat and clasped my hands.

My mother breathed deeply and rubbed the soreness out of her wrist.

"His name is Gregory Baker. I'm sorry I never told you that before, but that's the way he wanted it. He wouldn't even let Grandma Jean tell you."

"Why were you here three months ago?"

"I...I wanted to tell him I was getting married. I wanted...I just thought that he should know."

I didn't press the matter any further.

Catolby Correction Institution was a medium security prison reserved for violent convicts on good behavior. Or so I read from the informational packet. Now I at least knew that my father's crime or crimes were violent. I'm not sure if I wanted to know more. Is that where I got my so-called violent streak? Had I inherited it from my biological father? Of course, I never considered myself violent. In my mind, I just did what I had to do when it had to be done. And if what needed to be done included violence, so be it.

True to her word, Holly did not go any further into the facility than she needed to. I wandered the visitor's courtyard alone searching for a man I didn't know. I found him seconds later. Or at least I assumed it was him. It had to be. The man

was a taller, darker, more muscular version of me.

"Would you like to play a game of chess?" My father smiled at me and gestured toward a table where he'd already set up the game. I imagined meeting my father several times in my head. I imagined what he'd look like since I'd never even seen a picture, what he'd sound like, and what his first words to me would be. Never, in all my imaginings, were his first words asking to play a game.

I nodded at the man who was easily 6'6" and 300 pounds of solid muscle. Then we both sat down at the picnic-style table. I looked around at the other tables in the courtyard and saw sons, daughters, wives, maybe even brothers and sisters hugging their incarcerated loved ones, sharing pictures, or relating family stories. We were the only ones playing a board game.

"You can tell a lot about a man by the way he plays a game of chess," my father said as he made his first move. He adjusted his round glasses and waited for me to take my turn.

I didn't want to play chess. I wanted some answers. I wanted him to tell me all the things that Holly refused to reveal. I made two or three hasty moves in a row and within seconds he had me in check. When I tried to move my king to a safe place he said, "You can't move there. My knight is on g6."

"Well then, game over. You win."

"No, it's not over. There's a way out. You're just not seeing it. You're being blinded by emotion." I wanted to slam my fist on the table and clear the insipid chessboard. "You're angry with me. I can see it in your eyes. You can't let anger choose for you. You have to control it."

"You're a convicted felon and you're giving me advice about controlling my anger?"

"Maybe I'm *exactly* who should be giving you advice. I've gone down your path and it brought me to this place.

Hindsight is clearer than foresight, my son."

"Don't call me your son. I didn't even know your name before a few minutes ago. I know nothing about you and you know nothing about me." My father calmly pushed the chessboard to the side. He clasped his hands in front of him and sighed.

"I know more about you than you'll ever know. I know you're a scared little boy trying to be a man. I know you lash out at anything remotely threatening. I know you're highly intelligent, but you insist on using your fist instead of your mind." My father pointed to his temple for emphasis. "I know you're a sensitive soul who loves completely and who needs to be loved and needed in return. I know you love your mother and your baby sister more than yourself and you would give your life for them. And I know all these things, Garrett, because I was exactly the same way at your age. Do you know how much it pains your mother to see history repeating itself? To see my sins passed on to you? Do you know how many times she's told me that you remind her of me?"

"No, I *don't* know. Since I had no idea my mother was communicating with you I had no way of knowing." I crossed my arms over my chest.

"Don't be mad at your mother. I told her to keep it from you. I didn't want you to know who or what I was."

"So you don't want me, but you still want Holly."

My father bolted out of his seat causing several heads to turn in his direction.

"That's enough for today, Garrett. I'll see you next Saturday." He turned to walk away.

"Who says I'm coming back next Saturday?" My father turned back, rested his hands on the table, and in a calm, controlled voice said,

"You're coming back every Saturday or I'm not letting

Corbin adopt you."

***

"How was it?" My mother asked when I got into the car.

"Strange."

"Yeah, he can be that way sometimes." My mother smiled wistfully. She lost herself in a memory of some sort. A happy memory. It wasn't fair. I didn't have happy memories in which to lose myself. I was momentarily jealous of her reverie and wanted to snatch it away.

"Hol…mother, please. No more lies and mystery. Just tell me why he's in jail."

My mother's eyes glistened and her lips trembled as she said, "Murder."

"Murder? Whose murder? Whom did he kill?"

Before bursting into tears she said, "My father."

## Chapter 6:
## Tangled Web

My father killed my grandfather? That's why he was in jail? I was the child of a murderer. I felt my stomach twist and tighten. I tried to tell myself that it didn't matter. It didn't change who I was.

It shouldn't have been that much of a surprise, right? I knew he had to have committed some sort of felony to be serving a life sentence. Why did the fact that it was murder affect me so much? Why did the idea that he had murdered my grandfather make me so sick to my stomach?

"Are you all right, Garrett?" my mother asked after taking her eyes off the road for a moment. I nodded weakly unable to open my mouth to utter a sound. "You really don't look so good, baby. Do you need me to pull over?"

Holly didn't wait for a response. Instead, she crossed two lanes of traffic and pulled off onto the shoulder of the highway. I opened the door and let the bile that had been churning in my stomach flow out of me.

"I'm sorry I didn't tell you," she said as she rubbed my back and held my hair out of my face. "I didn't think...I didn't want..." My mother buried her face in my shoulder and wept softly.

I wiped my mouth on my sleeve. "Why do you still talk to him and visit him? How can you stand to look at him?

He killed your father, your flesh and blood."

"Things aren't always that simple, Garrett. Not everything is just black and white."

I tried to imagine what it would be like to lose your father at the hand of your lover. Or what kind of circumstances would cause you to murder your girlfriend's parent. My mother obviously still loved my father. There had to be an explanation, some key to unraveling the tangled web that was my parents' history. I needed to talk to someone, maybe someone in the family. But there was no one. As far as I knew, my parents didn't have siblings. My father's mother was dead and my mother's mother refused to even look at me.

I remember once when I was 12 and Eden was seven, my mother sent me to buy a few groceries. Nothing was strange in that alone, but I found it odd that Holly wouldn't let Eden come with me. Eden always went to the store with me. I used it as a time to quiz her on percents and proportions. I didn't argue, though. I just figured my mother wanted to do Eden's hair or something. As I walked back to the two bedroom duplex we rented at the time, I noticed a black Cadillac pulling away.

"Who was in the car?" I asked when I entered the house, setting the groceries on the kitchen table.

"Oh, Gary, you just missed Grandma," Eden blurted before my mother had a chance to think of a suitable lie. "Mommy, why didn't grandma want to meet Gary?" I locked eyes with my mother. Her silence profoundly answered Eden's question that words would not have accomplished. All these years I thought my grandmother's hate and rejection of me simply stemmed from my race. While that still may be part of the reason, being the son of the man who murdered her husband would surely add to it.

When we got home from the prison, my mother ran

upstairs and locked herself in her room for the rest of the evening. Eden found me in the hallway and temporarily sidetracked my desire to unravel my mother's past.

"Gary, you gotta see this!" She exclaimed as she grabbed my hand and pulled me into her room.

"Can it wait Eden? I'm really tired. I just want to sleep." Eden crossed her arms and pouted. I couldn't stand to see her disappointed. "Okay, Bug, what is it?"

"Look at these," she said with renewed vigor as she pointed to a pile of pictures on her bed. I picked up a few of them and studied the beautiful teenager with wild blonde hair dressed in a tight outlandish leather outfit with strategically placed rips and tears. "Don't I look gorgeous?"

"You? This is you?" I looked closer, and sure enough, the beautiful teenager was my 11-and-a-half year old sister. Heat rose into my collar. The clothing, the hair, the makeup was all completely inappropriate for a child. "Who took these?" I asked through gritted teeth.

"Are you mad, Gary? Don't be mad?" Eden pleaded. "I thought I looked pretty."

"Who took the pictures, Eden?"

"It was Dashanka." Dashanka was a Ukrainian photographer that worked with Corbin in his studio. She specialized in photographing pale sickly thin girls in clothing that only a handful of Europeans found attractive. I had no idea why she suddenly decided to photograph my sister.

I gathered the scattered photos off of Eden's bed then stormed to Corbin's office upstairs.

"What is this?" I asked throwing the pictures onto his desk. Corbin put down the magnifying glass he had been using to check his latest work for defects. He studied the pictures for a moment then said,

"Wow, these are actually pretty good." He gestured for me to sit, but I continued to stand.

"You mean you haven't seen them before?"

"Unh-uh. I guess that's what Eden was doing all day with Dashanka." Corbin leaned back in his desk chair and continued to peruse the pictures casually.

"Why weren't you keeping an eye on her?"

"Garrett, I had to work. I knew she was safe. She never left the building."

"This is child exploitation. These pictures are inappropriate." I slammed my fist into his desk.

"Now that's going a bit too far, Garrett. I admit the pictures make her look a little older than she is, but she's not naked or anything. I really think you're overreacting." Corbin looked at me and smiled slightly. His relaxed demeanor somehow managed to cool the hot anger that had erupted in me. Corbin always had the ability to diffuse tense situations and make people feel comfortable. Models loved working with him because unlike some photographers, he never yelled or belittled them or their body image.

"What's going to happen to these pictures? Will they be published?"

"No, I think Dashanka was just playing around. These were probably just for fun. You can relax. No one else will ever see them." Corbin studied the pictures more closely. He picked up his magnifying glass and continued his examination. I stared at the top of his dark hair with the frosted blond tips. And though I didn't agree with men dyeing their hair for aesthetic purposes, the style worked for him and easily made him look ten years younger. "You have to admit. These are quite good. Your sister has a natural talent. The camera loves her." I looked at one of the pictures again. I could see what he meant. Her beauty was undeniable.

"She's too young," was my only retort.

"You're absolutely right. She's too young for pictures like this, but what about other pictures, more innocent ones."

"I don't know if I want my sister to be a model. I'm not sure it's safe." Corbin nodded acknowledging my concern.

"How about this, I'll let you and your mother see every photo taken of her before it gets published. Anything you don't agree with gets trashed, no questions."

"I'll think about it," I said reluctantly. I trusted Corbin, not my usual reaction to the men in Holly's life. The way he considered my feelings and took into account my need to protect Eden comforted me. He took me seriously. None of my mother's other partners ever did.

"So, how did your visit with your father go?" he asked with concern in his dark eyes. I shrugged. "I'm sorry you had to go through that, but it's the only way he'll let me adopt you."

"Why do you want to adopt me so badly anyway?" I settled in the chair in front of Corbin's desk. It was a question I'd been dying to ask, but never had the opportunity. We never really spoke one on one a lot. Corbin sighed then pushed his work away.

"I was an only child," he began. "My mother died in childbirth and my father died when I was 13. I was raised by my father's sister. I always wanted a family. I know how hard it is growing up without one. I know what a troubled life you and Eden have had. When I fell in love with your mother, I fell in love with the two of you as well. I want to see you happy. I want us to be a family, a happy family, the kind of family none of us have ever had." Corbin stood, walked around his desk then sat on the corner of it. "I know you'll never admit it, but I think you want a family as much as I do. You want to belong. I want to give you that."

I still had a hard time believing someone wanted me. The last time I felt truly wanted and loved was when I lived with my grandmother. Now, in the same day, I had my biological father and my stepfather professing their

respective desires to be a permanent part of my life. I should have been overjoyed. I should have felt as though the threads of pain and lies that restricted my growth and freedom were being unwound but instead, I felt even more trapped.

## Chapter 7:
## Sickness and Death

Monday morning before third period I waited at my locker for Maddie. We agreed that we would do the interview then since I had a free period and she had journalism class.

I missed her. I know it sounds ridiculous since I'd only met her once, but I missed her. I missed the conversations we could be having, the time we could be spending together and the embraces we could be sharing if only we knew each other better. I wanted that process to begin as soon as possible. The sooner I got to know her, the sooner those imagined conversations and embraces would become reality.

"Hi, Garrett," she said when she arrived. After the stressful weekend I'd had, I really needed to hear her voice. But something was wrong. Her voice sounded weak and strained. Nothing like I'd dreamed about all weekend. And when I looked into her normally radiant blue eyes, my heart raced with fear. They seemed dull and sallow.

"Are you okay, Maddie?"

"Why? Do I not look okay? God, I knew I should have worn makeup. I...I need to sit down."Maddie dropped her backpack, slammed her back against the locker and slid down to the ground.

"Are you sick? You're sick, aren't you?" What a senseless question. I could look at her and tell she was sick. I

couldn't think of anything else to say.

"I was a little sick over the weekend, but I'm better now. I want to do the interview." I squatted in front of her and felt her forehead.

"Maddie, you're burning up. Let me take you to the nurse." I took her hand in mine to help her up but she gripped it tightly and held me in place.

"No, no, I'm fine. It's just a cold. I just…just let me sit here for a while. Will you stay with me?"

"Yeah, sure." I sat next to her on the floor with her hand still in mine as the bell rang starting third period. Maddie took deep slow breaths and focused on a point in front of her on the floor.

I stared at our entwined fingers. The contrast of my dark caramel colored skin to her creamy vanilla made my heart flutter. Her hand was so tiny and fit perfectly into mine, like it was made to be there. I wished I could kiss each and every delicate little finger and take her pain away, but I thought that would be too presumptuous of me. So, I sat there holding her hand for an eternity.

Curiosity and concern ate away at me, but I didn't want to invade her privacy. A part of me really didn't even want to ask what was going on. I had enough questions in my life I didn't want to add more. I just wanted to sit next to her and enjoy the feel of her hand in mine. But I also didn't want to sit there without talking. She might think I didn't like her. So, I started talking.

"When I was little, my grandmother used to have me learn a word a day. By the time I was five, I had the vocabulary beyond that of most 12- year-olds according to the tests anyway. The odd thing is, I enjoy learning, but I don't like school. Never have. I think it's a waste of time. My seventh grade Algebra teacher used to make me stand in the back of the classroom because I would fall asleep every day."

I smiled and looked over at Maddie who concentrated on her breathing. I fell silent again for a few moments wondering if she had asthma. Something deep inside me wished I would have to give her mouth to mouth resuscitation. I shook off that thought then said, "I don't think I could pick a favorite or most meaningful word if you paid me. The closest would probably be…bereft – adjective, lacking something needed or expected." I sighed. That would certainly describe my life. I didn't even know what it was I lacked, but there was definitely something missing in my life. "Definition two, suffering the death of a loved one. It was the word I learned the day after my grandmother died."

Maddie looked at me for the first time in half an hour.

"Thank you for sharing that with me. And thank you for not treating me like some sort of leper or berating me with questions. I get so sick of explaining it sometimes." Explaining what, I thought. Maddie tried to stand and I helped her to her feet. Then her cell phone rang. "Hello," she answered. "Yes, daddy…no…I'm fine daddy…I *am* in class, kinda. I'm doing an interview…I don't know. Okay." She put her phone down and asked me, "Would you take my pulse please?" I nodded as I reached for her wrist. She stared into my eyes as she grabbed my hand and placed it on her neck. When I finished, she put the phone back to her ear. "About 112…a friend…he's really smart, daddy I think he knows how to check a pulse…no, he's just a friend…I'm fine, I want to stay in school…no…no…okay…I love you, too." Maddie closed her phone.

"Do you need me to do anything?"

"No, I'm gonna go home." Maddie grabbed both my hands and swung them side to side.

I should have kissed her right then and there. It was the perfect opportunity. We were alone, holding hands, and staring into each other's eyes. But, she had just called me her

'friend.' Maybe she only saw me as a friend. I didn't want to embarrass myself so, instead of kissing her, I said, "Do you want me to take you?"

"No, my dad's sending the driver." I thought I noted disappointment in her eyes. Did she want to kiss me as well?

"I guess we'll have to reschedule the interview." I smiled down at her.

"Definitely." She smiled back.

***

"Are you okay, Gary?" Eden asked while we ate lunch.

"Yeah, why?"

" ' cause you look rather *despondent*," she said proudly. I couldn't help but smile at her correct usage of the word of the day.

"I'm not *despondent*, Bug. I'm fine."

Eden wrinkled her nose. "Is it about that girl, Marty, Marjorie…"

"Maddie," I offered. Eden shrugged and took a bite of her hamburger. "I guess I am a little *despondent* over her," I added after thinking for a moment. She seemed really sick. I wondered what was wrong with her and why she thought I would treat her like a leper. I hoped it wasn't anything life-threatening.

"Why?" Eden asked as she wiped her mouth on a napkin. "Does she not like you or something?"

"I don't know."

"If she doesn't like you, she's insane. You're the sweetest, cutest, smartest boy I know. And you're the best big brother in the world." My heart smiled. "Do you want me to talk to her?" she added.

"Thanks for the offer, Eden, but I think I can handle it." I tousled her hair and stole a french fry.

\*\*\*

That night, Maddie called me. We spoke for hours about nothing at all and it was wonderful. I didn't worry about secrets, lies, and murders. We talked about movies, books, magazines. We even debated over which is the better side item, onion rings or french fries. In Maddie's opinion, circular food of any kind wins hands down. Maddie was the first person ever to make me laugh, besides Eden of course.

"Gary, I need help with my homework," Eden called as she entered my room. I covered the phone with my hand and said,

"Can we do it later, Bug? I'm on the phone."

"You said that two hours ago."

"Just ten…twenty more minutes okay? I promise." Eden left my room in a huff.

"Who was that?" Maddie asked.

"That's just my baby sister. She needs help with her homework."

"Oh, well, do you need to go?"

"No…no, I want to talk to you."

An hour later, I went to Eden's room.

"Okay, are you ready to get started?" I asked, hopping on her bed.

"Don't worry about it, Gary. Corbin helped me." Eden had already changed into her pajamas and was tying her long hair into a ponytail.

"He did?"

"Yeah, I had to write this paper about some stupid lizard and Corbin helped me write it and even found some pictures for me to add."

"Oh, okay. So, you're all done then?"

"Yep." Eden crawled into bed and pulled the covers up

to her chin.

"What about math? Did you do your math homework?"

"Yep." Eden rolled onto her side, turning her back towards me.

"Eden." She didn't respond. "Eden, are you mad at me?" She continued to ignore me. "I asked you a question, little girl," I said, as I started tickling her. She laughed and kicked and squealed and begged me to stop. "Not until you forgive me."

"I forgive you, I forgive you," she panted.

"Good. I love you. See you in the morning." I kissed her forehead then stood up to leave.

"Gary," she called before I reached the door. "Do you love *her* too?" I knew she meant Maddie.

"I think so."

"Well, then I'll love her, too, okay?" I smiled and clicked off her light.

## Chapter 8:
## Beautiful

"I'm cold," Eden said for the fifth time. "I think it's gonna snow."

"It's not going to snow," I said, feeling she was being a little dramatic.

"I hope it does snow. Maybe they'll send us home or cancel school tomorrow. Why are we standing outside, anyway? Who are you looking for?" She whined.

"Don't end sentences with prepositions." I stated as I stared at the cars pulling into the parking lot of Barton Arms. I knew Maddie would be arriving any minute.

"Fine. Who are you looking for, *Gary*?"

"Very funny. Go to class. We can meet for lunch today, okay?" I kissed the side of her head and tousled her hair. Eden re-adjusted the purple beret Corbin brought her from Paris last week, lifted her chin in the air and strutted off as if she was mad at me.

"I'll see you for lunch." I called, ignoring her façade.

"I love you!" She replied brightly as she blew me a kiss and ran away. She couldn't even pretend to be angry with me for more than a few seconds.

I leaned against the railing and tried to assume a relaxed position so Maddie wouldn't think I was waiting for her. Seconds later, she appeared.

"Hey," I said when she was about to walk past me.

"Hello." Maddie hugged her books tightly, adjusted her backpack and avoided making eye contact.

"Can I carry those for you?"

"Why don't you go carry *her* books?" she said looking in the direction Eden had just walked.

"She's in middle school. She barely has any books."

"Middle school? You're dating a middle schooler? That's sick, Garrett!" She started up the steps, but I grabbed her arm and turned her around.

"Wait, Maddie. She's my sister. That's Eden." I could see the wave of confusion wash over her face. "I thought I told you she was white."

"*That's* your sister?" I nodded. "My God, I'm such an idiot. I…I saw you eating lunch with her yesterday and then I saw you holding her hand and I just assumed. Oh, my God, I am a complete moron."

"Is that why you've been avoiding me?" We hadn't spoken since our three hour phone conversation Monday night. I'd wave to her in the hall and she'd turn away or slip into a classroom. She was killing me, literally killing me. I couldn't get her out of my mind. All I wanted to do was see her or talk to her or just touch her hand again.

"She doesn't look twelve or almost twelve," Maddie said after licking her lips. "She's…she's stunning. I mean, really, how tall is she? 5'7", 5'8"? No wonder your stepfather wants her to model. When I saw you with her I thought, why would he want me when he could have her? But she's your sister." Maddie chuckled a little. "But you can see why I was jealous. She…she's gorgeous. I should have known. I mean, look at you. You're beautiful so of course your sister would be beautiful."

She thought I was beautiful? Of course, I'd heard girls refer to me as 'sexy' or 'cute' or whatever, but something

66

about the way she called me 'beautiful' touched me. I suddenly felt flushed and nervous. I hid my anxiety by smiling confidently and saying, "You think I'm beautiful?" Maddie turned red and dropped all of her books. Then she swallowed hard and licked her lips again. She did that a lot. I think it was a nervous habit. She didn't realize it, but that habit drove me insane with desire. I loved her lips. Maddie started applying some cherry lip gloss that she'd retrieved from her coat pocket while I picked up her books. I saw an opportunity.

"Can I try some?"

"Lip gloss?" she asked completely confused.

"Yeah, just a little." Maddie shrugged and held the tube out to me. But instead of taking it, I leaned down and caressed her lips with mine. They were even softer than I'd imagined. Her touch sent electric warmth careening through my body. She kissed me back. She wrapped her arms around my neck and pressed me closer to her. "Can I take you somewhere? Today after school…can we go somewhere…together?"

"Anywhere," she breathed.

***

During lunch I tried to find her. I thought maybe we could grab a bite together. I ended up in front of the newspaper office.

"Is it true you kissed that genius black kid?" I heard a girl ask before I entered. I knew she had to be talking to Maddie. I stood outside the door and listened for her response.

"His name is Garrett," she said.

"Oh my God, so it is true?" The girl squealed. "What was it like?"

"It was…it was perfect. I mean I've kissed before, but nothing like this. I seriously almost fell over." I relished in the fact that Maddie had enjoyed the encounter as well. My lips involuntarily curved into a smile of satisfaction.

"So, are you guys like together now?"

"I don't know."

"You know your father's gonna flip, right?"

"My father doesn't have to know."

"Ha! How long do you think you can hide it from him? The senator has eyes everywhere. I wouldn't be surprised if he already knows."

So, Maddie's father was a senator that apparently wouldn't approve of me. I decided to use my lunch period for some investigation into this matter. But on my way to the computer lab, I ran into Eden.

"There you are, Gary. I've been looking all over for you." Eden jumped on my back and kissed me on the cheek.

"You have? Why?"

She jumped down, tilted her head to the side and stared at me. She looked rather confused as she said, "You said we were having lunch today."

"I did? That's right. I'm sorry, Bug. I forgot."

"You forgot about me?" Eden's voice quivered a little.

"No, of course not. Look, we have twenty minutes left. Let's go get a sandwich or something, okay?"

"Okay." Eden wound her fingers in mine as we walked to the cafeteria.

\*\*\*

"Hi," I smiled when Maddie walked up to my locker after school.

"Hi," she responded. All day I'd rehearsed what I would to say to her, but now that she stood in front of me, all words and reasonable thought eluded me. I leaned down awkwardly and kissed her on the cheek. Maddie blushed and tucked a blond curl behind her ear. Then we just stared into each other's eyes until Eden came and squealed, "Garieeeee!" as she tackled me with a hug.

I hugged her back briefly then said, "Eden, this is Maddie."

"Hi, Maddie," Eden said as she let go of me and hugged Maddie as well. "So this is the girl with the eyes you want to drown in," she said to me. Eden placed the back of her hand on her forehead and faked a swoon. Maddie turned red and stared at her shoes.

"Don't end sentences with prepositions. How many times do I have to tell you that?" I tickled her until she promised to never do it again. "Eden, Maddie and I are going to go grab a cup of coffee. Why don't you call Corbin and ask him to pick you up? He's at the studio right now so he's not that far away." Eden stopped laughing and stared at me.

"What?" she asked sharply.

"I said, I'm taking Maddie for coffee."

"But, it's Wednesday," she said with hurt in her eyes. "Wednesday is library day. You have to pick out my book for the week."

"I know I usually take you to the library on Wednesdays, but I thought, just this once, that I could go out with Maddie for a little while."

"Garrett, if you want to take your sister to the library, I'll understand," Maddie offered. I looked from Maddie to Eden and back to Maddie. I felt like I had to choose between them. I wanted to make them both happy. I wanted to spend time with each of them. I thought about that warm soft kiss I'd shared with Maddie that morning and my body involuntarily chose her over Eden. I didn't know the devastating effects that choice would make in all our lives.

\*\*\*

Maddie and I sat on the same side of the booth letting our coffee get cold as we kissed each other.

"I'm so sorry I thought you were dating your sister," she said for the hundredth time once I let her up for air. "You must think I'm a complete idiot."

"I don't do this to idiots," I said as I nuzzled her neck. She smelled so good. Like a combination of soap and cherries.

"And what exactly are you doing?"

"I'm checking your pulse." Maddie flung her head back and erupted into adorable giggles. I kissed up the side of her neck to her earlobe then found her lips again.

I could feel people in the coffee shop staring at us, but I didn't care. I needed this. I needed her. I couldn't remember a time when I felt so happy, so free, so complete. I wasn't going to let anything ruin it, especially a cell phone.

Maddie jolted when it rang. She pulled away from me and searched for her purse. When she couldn't find it, she dumped the contents out on the table.

"Damn it, where is it?" she mumbled as she rummaged through her scattered belongings. The phone continued to ring as Maddie grew more and more frantic. Why was she in such a panic?

I reached behind her, picked up her coat, and pulled her cell phone out of the pocket. As soon as she saw it, she snatched it out of my hand, opened it and said, "Hi Daddy." She mouthed 'thank you' then scooted away from me. "That's because I'm not at school…I went to Java Joe's with a friend…I know what caffeine can do to me…I know…I got decaf…you are? Okay…okay…I love you too." She hung up and looked at her watch.

"Is everything all right?" I asked. Something about the way Maddie talked with her father made me nervous. He seemed a bit controlling.

"Yeah, yeah, everything's fine. Um, I need to go," she said as she waited for me to slide out of the booth.

"Maddie, I'm worried about you. What's going on? Are you afraid of your father? Is he hurting you?"

"No, Garrett, it's nothing like that. You've got the wrong idea. He's just really...protective when it comes to me. I swear I'll explain everything soon, just not now. He'll be here any second." Maddie glanced at the door nervously. I wasn't convinced. I knew something wasn't right. This guy was going to have to go through me to get to Maddie again.

I rooted myself in the seat blocking her exit and crossed my arms. "I think I want to meet this guy."

"Please, Garrett, not today." Maddie took my chin in her hands and turned my face toward her. She paralyzed me with her deep blue eyes as she said, "If you care for me at all, you'll trust me." What could I do? I did care for her. I'd only known her for a few days and I cared for her more than I could ever imagine. I slid out of the seat and let her out. She gathered her belongings then ran towards the door. After a few steps, she stopped, turned and ran back to me. She stood on her tiptoes, wrapped her arms around my neck and kissed me deeply. Then she dashed out of the coffee shop and into a waiting town car.

An uneasy feeling developed in the pit of my stomach. Maddie needed help. She needed me. I wanted to protect her and take away the pain that had obviously enveloped her life. My problems didn't matter anymore. All that mattered was Maddie.

# Chapter 9:
# Silent Devotion

As I made the 30 minute walk from Barton Arms to Corbin's studio, thoughts of Maddie overflowed my mind.

*Was she all right?*
*Did she think of me?*
*When would I next see her*
*So I could again be free?*

Corbin's studio was located about two blocks north of DuPont Circle in Washington DC. He often did photo shoots on location, but this week he was working on a special layout for Gap and I knew he would be in his studio.

Corbin wasn't terribly famous, but his excellent rapport with models had helped to boost his career into a more elite realm. Three years ago, he only did work for catalog companies like Wal-Mart, JC Penney, and Sears. But about a year ago, he started receiving calls from Gap, Old Navy, American Eagle, and Abercrombie and Fitch.

Then, a few months ago, Donna Karan requested him for a layout for Vogue magazine and nothing has been the same since. He opened this studio in DC and travels to exotic cities like Paris, Rome, and Milan. I even heard rumors of a possible reality show on TLC. I was happy for him; he was a nice guy and deserved success. I just hoped his new found fame wouldn't affect me and Eden.

Before I reached the studio, I stopped at Barnes and Noble to pick up a book of poetry for Eden. I wanted to make amends. I thought for sure she would be upset with me for choosing to spend time with Maddie instead of her. I thought wrong.

"What is this?" I asked Corbin's secretary Courtney. It was a pretty stupid question since I could clearly see for myself.

Eden, still dressed in her Barton Arms uniform, posed, smiled and flirted with the camera as Corbin snapped picture after picture.

"Your sister is incredible," Courtney said. "It looks like she's been doing this for years."

"Why is he...how did this happen?"

"The model for the Gap shoot was late so Corbin just started taking pictures of Eden. I really think she's gonna work out better for the layout. I mean look at the connection between them. Isn't he amazing?" Courtney didn't take her eyes off of Eden and Corbin. I couldn't tell whether she was more amazed by Eden's beauty or Corbin's technique with a camera. Courtney was an art major at Georgetown who wanted to be a photographer one day so she absolutely idolized Corbin.

I looked again at Corbin immortalizing my sister with a camera. Surprisingly, I wasn't angry. I felt relieved. The clothing wasn't inappropriate, plenty of people were around, and Eden looked happy. Genuinely happy. I waved to her so that she would know I was there, and then I slipped into Corbin's office and called Maddie.

Maddie and I spent almost every free moment together. In the mornings we'd meet at the coffee shop and walk to school. During our common free period, we'd take a

stroll around campus together no matter how cold it was outside. She offered to join Eden and me for one of our frequent trips to the library or local museum, but suddenly, Eden didn't want to go anymore.

Due to some sort of security breach, my father's prison had suspended visitation for the week. So instead of driving to North Carolina to see him, I took a few minutes and spoke to him on the phone. Then I met Maddie in the city where we caught a movie together. I guess she quickly became my girlfriend. I'd never had a girlfriend before. I don't know why. I guess I had always been too preoccupied with taking care of Holly and Eden that I really didn't have time to think of my own wants and needs. Now that they were happy, I too, had a chance to be happy.

The next Wednesday, Maddie and I went to the library. She politely asked Eden to come along, but once again, Eden refused.

"I can't believe your favorite book is a dictionary," Maddie said jokingly as she sat on my lap in the reference section.

"Shhh," I said, placing a finger on her lips. "This is a library, you know," I whispered. "Besides, it's not just any dictionary. It's the OED. It not only gives you the definitions, it gives you the etymologies, and the transformations of the words over time. It's quite amazing."

"You're amazing." She kissed me and added, "If you weren't so sweet and cute and sexy, I would think you were the biggest nerd in the world." She smiled and leaned in to kiss me again, but her phone rang. I had gotten used to that bothersome intrusion over the past week. Anytime we got remotely intimate, that stupid phone rang. It was almost as if her father knew the exact moment to call in order to keep us from getting too close.

Maddie hopped off my lap and darted out of the

library while simultaneously digging her phone out of her purse. As I gathered my books and followed her, I noticed the librarian staring at me. I didn't know why she stared. It could have been the usual. She didn't like to see an interracial couple. Or, with Maddie running out of the door in a hurry, she could have thought I'd hurt her somehow.

I never got used to the suspicion aroused from a black man with a white woman, or girl for that matter. Once when Eden was eight or nine, she fell and busted her lip while we were at the park. I tried to clean her up and calm her down as she cried hysterically. When the police officer first approached us, I thought he just wanted to help, but in a few moments it became clear he thought I was a threat to Eden. It took thirty minutes and a call to our social worker to straighten out the situation.

Maddie sat outside on the front steps hugging her knees when I caught up with her.

"Do you need to go home?" I asked, as I placed her coat around her shoulders.

She shook her head. "Not really, he was just calling to say he's working late. He does that a lot. Works late. I think that's why he calls me like every half hour or whatever. It makes him feel like he's still my father and a part of my life or something."

I sat next to her and set our backpacks in front of me. I couldn't think of anything to say. Up until this point, Maddie and I had shied away from talking about our personal lives too much. I think we both sought each other as an escape from the demons that haunted us. This was the first time she'd said anything remotely specific about her father.

"Well, do you want to come to my house for a little while?" I asked, sensing that she really didn't want to be alone.

"Can I?"

The house was empty when we arrived. I assumed Holly, Eden, and Corbin were at Corbin's studio, but I really didn't dwell on it for too long. Instead, I thought about the fact that Maddie and I were alone, together, in my house. Alone. The excitement of that realization consumed me. I wondered if she felt the same. If she wanted me half as much as I wanted her, this was going to be a memorable afternoon.

"Um, do you want something to drink? Are you hungry? I can make you something. I'm a pretty good cook."

Maddie smiled, "I'm fine with water."

I went in the kitchen to pour her a glass of water. When I returned to the living room, she was gone. I found her lurking in the hallway.

"I assume this is your room," she said after she'd opened my door and stepped in.

"How can you tell?" I placed her glass on the dresser then wrapped my arms around her.

"I think the decor, or lack thereof, gives it away. I mean, I peeked into Eden's room and it's adorable. A little too purple for my taste, but adorable. This is just bland, bland, bland." She smiled and kissed me.

I had to admit, I hadn't put much effort into making this room really mine. I think something inside me felt I wouldn't be living in Corbin's house for too long. Things in my life just never went that well.

"You should let me decorate for you," she said between kisses. "Seriously, I saw the perfect comforter and curtains for you."

I lifted her up and placed her on top of the dresser as I continued to kiss her neck and ignore her ramblings about bedspreads. I really wanted to toss her on the bed and ravage her, but I didn't want to be too presumptuous. In the back of my mind, however, I hoped this kissing would lead to something else. I hoped that she had wandered into my

bedroom for a reason.

"They're perfect," she said, distracting me from my desires. "They're white with black words scrolled across. You can even have them custom made and get whatever words you want written on them. Since you love words so much, we can get some of your favorites on them. And since they're in black and white –." Maddie froze and breathed in sharply.

"What? What is it?" I pulled away from her and looked into her eyes.

"I mean, it doesn't have to be black and white. That's not why I thought of it. I thought you would like it because of the word thing that's all. I wasn't trying to imply anything about your race."

Why would she even think that? I wondered whether she was really with me for me, or if my race some sort of novelty for her. Or worse, was she dating a black guy just so she could upset her father and get attention from him? "Maddie, does my race bother you?"

"No, no not at all," she said quickly, too quickly. "I just want you to know that it doesn't matter to me. I don't want you to think that I care about it…'cause I don't. I just care about you and how you make me feel. I've never been happier than…than when I'm with you, Garrett."

The excitement of having her in my room quickly waned as I thought about the possibility of her feelings for me not being genuine. I began to doubt myself, to doubt her. A normal teenage boy probably wouldn't care, but I was not a normal teenage boy. I couldn't want someone who didn't want me.

I ran my fingers through my hair and turned away from her.

"Garrett," she said as she grabbed my arm and pulled me back to her. She wrapped her arms around my waist and

held me tightly while resting her head on my shoulder.

We stayed there, holding each other, speaking silent words of devotion for what seemed like forever. Then we both jumped at the sound of a car door. Maddie nearly fell off the dresser. We made it back to the living room just as Corbin opened the front door with Eden a step behind.

"Holly's not here?" Corbin asked as he set a bag of groceries on the kitchen table.

I shook my head. "I thought she was with you?"

"Nope. I haven't seen her all day. Eden's been helping me out at the studio all afternoon." Eden nodded her head slowly in agreement, while not taking her eyes off of Maddie. Soon an awkward silence fell as Corbin too began to stare at Maddie. I realized I hadn't introduced her or explained why she was there.

"I'm Garrett's friend, Maddie," she volunteered while extending her hand to Corbin.

Friend? Why did she keep calling me her friend?

## Chapter 10:
## Father Figure

As I got ready for school the next day, Eden came into my room and sat quietly on the floor. I knew she wanted to talk to me about something, but I thought it best to let her do so in her own time. I busied myself by organizing my backpack and making my bed, anything to waste time until Eden was ready to bring up what was on her mind.

For lack of anything else to do, I picked up my dictionary, sat on my bed, and began my search for the word of the day. Usually, I just opened the dictionary and randomly pointed to a word. Today, in order to prolong the process, I decided to actually look at the words and pick out a 'pretty' one just like Grandma Jean used to do. I smiled at the memory of her. I wondered if, wherever she was, she knew how much of an influence she'd had on my life. Would I have the same love of words if she hadn't instilled the value of them into me at such a young age? I still remembered how we would walk through the neighborhood hand in hand and she would point to signs and ask me to read them to her. I could have easily lied to her about what they said and made up my own thing, but I would never do that to Grandma Jean. I loved and respected her too much. She would also take me to libraries in rich neighborhoods where they would have story time for the kids. She put so much effort into trying to

make me a good and educated person. I hoped I'd never let her down.

I was lost in memories of my Grandmother when Eden said, "Garrett, am I too young to have a boyfriend?"

"Boyfriend?" I closed the dictionary and placed it on the bed trying to remain calm. I knew I would one day have to have this conversation with her, but I never thought it would be so soon. "Yes, you're too young. Why would you even ask that? You're 11 years old." The goal of remaining calm proved harder than I thought.

Eden hugged her knees and stared at her shoes. She frowned as if she had a secret she didn't want to share.

"Is there something you want to tell me? Did someone ask you out?"

"Well, Adam Roberts kinda asked me to the eighth grade dance and I kinda want to go with him." Eden looked up at me with her brown green eyes as if pleading with me to give her permission. I felt honored that she had asked me instead of Holly or Corbin. I guessed that over the years I felt like more of a parent to her than either one of them ever could.

I sighed, relieved that she was only concerned about some silly little middle school dance. I hoped I could delay the inevitable sex talk. It was a subject Holly should address with her, but I knew from experience that my mother didn't always do what she should do.

"Going to a dance with a boy doesn't mean you're boyfriend and girlfriend, Eden. It's just a date. One date is okay, but if he asks for anything more that's absolutely not okay."

Eden was pleased with this response. She stood up, kissed me on the cheek then skipped off to her bedroom probably to find something to wear to the dance even though it was more than a week away. I relaxed on my bed and

continued my search for a word of the day. I knew it would be at least another twenty minutes before Eden was ready to head off to school.

As I skimmed the pages, my mind began to wrestle with the idea of my baby sister going on dates. Even though it was just a dance that would be chaperoned by probably the most uptight set of faculty known to man, it was still a date. I was sixteen and *I* hadn't even had a real date. Though I hoped to change that soon with Maddie.

Then another thought entered my mind. This boy Adam was in the eighth grade. I was in the eighth grade when I lost my virginity. And why would an eighth grader want to go out with a sixth grader anyway?

I slammed the dictionary shut then stormed off to Eden's room.

I found her talking excitedly on the phone, probably with Tracee, her best friend.

"Can I talk to you for a minute?" I sat next to her on her bed trying to think of the best way to phrase my words. I knew she wouldn't be happy with me to say the least.

"Okay, Tray, I'll see you at school and I'll show you a picture of the dress. I borrowing it from one of the models at my dad's studio," she said into the phone before hanging up.

Her dad's studio? She now considered Corbin her dad? I didn't know how I felt about that. I was glad that she had a father figure in her life and that she was comfortable enough with Corbin to call him dad. I couldn't even do that with my own biological father. But that could've been because of deeper psychological reasons. After all I had been through with the men in Holly's life, I didn't know if I would ever be able to trust a man enough to call him dad.

Eden crossed her legs Indian style and stared up at me expectantly waiting for what was so important that I would interrupt a conversation with Tracee.

"I've been thinking and I've changed my mind."

"About what?"

"About the dance. I don't think you should go."

"You changed your mind? From like 30 seconds ago? What do you mean you changed your mind?" Eden hopped off the bed and confronted me.

"I just think you should wait until you're a little older. There will be plenty of time for dances later." I kept my voice as calm and even as possible.

"But, Garrett, you already said yes. I already told Tracee. She's so excited that I'm going to be the only sixth grader at the eighth grade dance. I was the only sixth grader invited. I have to go!" Tears of anger and disappointment welled in her eyes. I couldn't really comprehend why this meant so much to her. I guessed it was a girl thing.

"I'm sorry. You can't go." I remained calm, but my voice was firm.

"You can't do this to me. I'll ask mom. She'll let me go." She started toward the door. I jumped off the bed and blocked her exit.

"Not if I tell her not to. Holly trusts me. She'll agree with me."

Eden stomped her foot and crossed her arms knowing that I was right. Holly always deferred to me when it came to important decisions.

She sulked for a moment probably trying to think of her next move. She was not one to give up so easily. "Well then I'll ask Richard," she said finally. "He's the one that suggested I have a boyfriend. He thinks it'll be good for me. I'll get him to tell Holly that going to the dance is part of my therapy."

"Richard wants you to have a boyfriend? What does he have to do with this?"

"Mommy will believe a doctor over you," she

responded, avoiding my question.

The fact that Richard was starting to get involved in how I raised my sister incensed me. This was not my Eden being so openly defiant toward me. Someone had poisoned her and Richard seemed to be the obvious culprit. I would have to have a little chat with him at the very next opportunity. But right then, I had to deal with Eden.

"I said you're not going and that's final." I stared into her eyes as I towered over her.

My intimidation technique worked a little too well because Eden burst into tears. "Why do you hate me?" She sobbed.

I wrapped my arms around her and said, "I don't hate you, Bug. I'm doing this because I love you. I just want to protect you." She continued to cry. "You believe me don't you?"

She nodded as she wiped tears away. "I believe you. I'm sorry, Garrett. I just wanted to have what you have with Maddie. I want someone to love me the way you love her."

"There'll be plenty of time for that later, okay? Just be a kid for now, for as long as you can."

I wanted to wrap my sister in a magic bubble that would keep her eleven years old forever. But time and unforeseen occurrences were about to thrust her into cruel maturity.

# Chapter 11:
# Mortality

When we got to school that morning, I met Maddie in front of her locker.

"I missed you," I said after a kiss hello.

"I missed you, too." She blushed.

"Do you want to go to Java Joe's after school today?"

"I guess…we can…if you want…but…" She looked at her shoes. She seemed nervous. Something was wrong.

"Can you not go? If you don't want to we don't have to. I just wanted to be with you."

"No, it's not that. I want to, I definitely want to spend time with you," she said quickly as she looked up at me. "It's just that…" She looked down again and started wringing her hands. "I just had something else in mind. Um, my father left for Boston this morning and he won't be back until Monday and so I have the place to myself so I just wanted to know if you wanted to, you know, come over or something, but you don't have to or anything, I was just wondering. I thought we could watch a movie or something, but if you would rather get coffee that's fine. Or if you don't like movies or something, that's fine too. I mean we can go to the library again if you want. It was just a thought."

I leaned down and kissed her so passionately I thought I felt her knees buckle.

"What time do you want me there?"

\*\*\*

"Where are you going?" Eden asked that evening as I got ready.

"I'm going to see Maddie," I said as I dabbed on some aftershave.

"Again? She must be really special." Eden came into my bedroom and sat on my bed.

"She is special. But not as special as you." I walked to the bed and kissed the top of her head.

"Really?" Eden smiled.

"Of course." I sat down next to her and slipped on my shoes.

"Can I brush your hair? Remember when we used to brush each other's hair every night? Why don't we do that anymore?" Eden sat on her knees and started running her fingers through my hair.

"I don't know, Bug. I guess we just grew out of it. We can start it again tomorrow if you want, but right now I have to go. I have to catch the metro all the way back to DC and it's already six."

"Oh, okay," she said as she sat back down on the bed and crossed her legs Indian style.

"Are you upset with me?" I asked when I saw the sad look in her eyes.

"No…yes…a little, I guess."

"I'm so sorry, Eden." I hugged her. "I'll make it up to you, I promise. How about Sunday you and I spend the whole day together? We can see some museums, have lunch then go to a movie, okay?"

"Okay," she said, her mood brightening.

"Now, go do your homework and read that book of

85

poetry I bought you. I'll try to be back in time to tuck you in to bed."

"I love you, Gary. And I'm glad she makes you happy. You deserve to be happy."

\*\*\*

Maddie actually had two homes. She had a three story mansion in McLean, VA and a five bedroom condominium in DC near embassy row. That night at seven, I met her at the condo. When I got there, she had popcorn, chips, and brownies out on the table. She also had several DVD's picked out for me to peruse. So she really did want to watch a movie. I had to admit, I felt a little disappointed.

"The brownies are organic and sugar-free. It's all we have." She admitted. "But I can send out for some different ones if you want." She took my coat and hung it on a hanger.

"I'm sure these will be fine." I said as I looked around her elegant home. The furniture looked antique and expensive. I didn't want to touch anything for fear I would diminish its value. I think Maddie noticed my discomfort.

"You can have a seat if you like." She smiled and gestured for the couch. "Oh, um, let me get you something to drink." Maddie dashed off to the kitchen as I sat on the couch.

"You're still in your uniform," I said when she came back holding two glasses. I felt overdressed in my khakis and button down shirt. I actually borrowed a tie from Corbin. What was I thinking?

"Oh, yeah, I didn't have time to change. I actually just got here. I had a doctor's appointment after school. The maid set up the snacks and everything for us before she left for the day." Maddie handed me a glass then took a sip out of hers as if that's all she wanted to say about it. I gulped down the orange juice for lack of anything else to do. "Do you want some more?"

"No, I'm fine," I said setting the empty glass on the table in front of us. Time ticked on through our awkward silence as Maddie started to nervously tap her glass. Why didn't I just lean over and kiss her?

"So, your dad's gone for the weekend?" I asked finally. She smiled meekly and nodded all the while continuing to tap on her glass. Another silence fell. "Um, Maddie?"

"Huh?"

"Why are you so nervous?"

"Oh my God, is it that obvious? I'm such an idiot." Maddie bolted off the couch and tried to retreat into the kitchen, but I stood and touched her hand. When I turned her toward me, she got off balance and spilled her drink all over my shirt. "Oh, my God, oh my God, I'm so stupid. I didn't mean…here." She took off her sweater and started dabbing my chest.

"It's fine. I'm okay. It's just a little orange juice. No big deal."

"I can wash it for you. Just let me…" She started to unbutton my shirt.

"Don't!" I almost yelled as I grabbed her wrists. Maddie's lips quivered and tears instantly welled in her magnificent eyes. What kind of a monster was I to raise my voice to her? I just couldn't let her take off my shirt.

I pulled her close to me and let her cry.

"I'm such a loser. I wanted this to be special, but instead I'm a total spaz and I spilled juice on you and now you don't even want me to touch you."

"Oh, God, Maddie, it's not you. It's…" I lifted her chin and stared into those pools of blue. I wiped her tears away with my thumbs then planted a soft kiss on her lips. She smiled through the tears and warmed my soul. She slowly

melted away the emotional barriers I'd developed. Barriers that needed to come down once and for all.

I took her hand, sat her back down on the couch and said, "It's not that I don't want you to touch me. You have no idea how much I want that. I'm just afraid that if you know…that if you see…that if you get too close to me, the truth will scare you away." Maddie looked confused. The only way for her to understand would be to show her. I unbuttoned my shirt. When I opened it fully, she gasped and covered her mouth.

"Garrett, what happened to you?"

I pulled my shirt closed in shame. I didn't want to go into the whole story, but it was too late now. She'd already seen the abuse.

"When I was nine," I began, "my mother dated this guy who tried to rape her, but I was there to protect her. I stabbed him with a knife." My mind flashed back to the scene. I saw the blood streaming down his leg. I felt the pain of the broken arm he caused.

"After that," I continued, "my therapist and social worker thought it would be best if we didn't have knives in our house. She took them away. I was defenseless. About a year later, Eden's father came back into our lives.

"Joel had always hated me. I knew that. But he fed my mother a few lines about how he'd changed and she believed him. One night, my mother was at work. Eden was on the couch sleeping next to Joel as he watched TV. I sat in the corner just watching him. I wanted to make sure Eden was safe. I remember a lit ember from his cigarette fell and burned his bare chest."

I paused. Maddie placed my hands in hers once she noticed they were shaking. "He looked at me and accused me of laughing at him. 'You think that's funny, nigger?' he said. I told him I wasn't laughing, but he didn't believe me. Then he held the lit cigarette above Eden and said 'I bet you won't think it's funny if it happened to your sister'."

Maddie inhaled sharply. I didn't want to finish the story. I hadn't told anyone about this, not even Richard. Somehow I had managed to bury this episode into the deep recesses of my mind. I took deep slow breaths in order to continue without breaking down.

"I wanted to kill him. I wanted to strangle the life out of him with my bare hands. I wanted to slice out his heart. He made me choose. It was either Eden or me. I couldn't let him hurt my sister. He took that cigarette and burned me over and over and over. And then he lit another one and did it again." My voice leapt an octave, but I set aside the pain.

"Oh Garrett." Maddie placed my head on her shoulder and held me.

"I didn't cry. I never cried about it. I didn't want to give that bastard the satisfaction of knowing that he…" I couldn't hold it in any longer. Violent tears rushed forth from my body in powerful spasms.

"It's okay to cry, Garrett. You have to let it out sometime. You can't hold something like that in. It'll eat away at your soul until nothing is left."

I cried for a long time. Too long. I felt weak and pitiful. As soon as possible, I dried my eyes and forced my breathing to return to normal. I sat up and rubbed the back of my neck.

"I'm damaged goods. I'm nothing, nobody. I have to be for someone to do that to me, right?"

"No, don't say that, Garrett. You're wounded, but wounds heal." Maddie turned my face to hers. "I want to show you something," she said as she unbuttoned her shirt. She opened it and revealed a thick scar down the center of her chest. She placed my hand between her breasts and said, "I had a heart transplant when I was 14. That's why my dad is so overprotective and why I had that episode that Monday

at school and why I'm so nervous around you all the time. I've spent most of my life in and out of hospitals and haven't had a chance to talk to many boys." Maddie brought my hand to her lips then entwined our fingers. "So, we're both wounded, but we can heal each other."

"So, are you okay now? Are you healthy?"

"For the most part. My body has adjusted well to the heart. I still have to take a truckload of medications every day. Sometimes I have bad days, like Monday. I was pretty weak. I'm on a new prescription."

I tucked a blond curl behind her ear then caressed her cheek. "I'm glad you're okay." I kissed her gently. "I don't want to think…what if you…" Maddie silenced the thought with a kiss that made my entire body groan.

She scooted closer to me and crawled into my lap. My hands slid under her shirt and caressed her back. Her kisses deepened.

"I want you so badly," I said into her neck.

She pulled away from me flushed and breathing heavily. She gave me a wide-eyed stare. I thought I'd scared her. I thought I was moving too fast. I thought wrong. She stood, grabbed my hand, and slowly led me down a hallway.

The moonlight spilling through the French doors of the balcony in her bedroom set a perfect romantic mood. Maddie gently closed the door behind her then led me to the bed.

"Maddie, what are you −" She placed her finger over my lips.

"You don't know how good it feels to have someone want me and not pity me." She twirled a lock of my hair around her finger for a second then said, "For six years, I've spent my life thinking about my death. The day I met you in front of your locker was the first time I could remember when I wasn't fixated on my own mortality. All I could think about was when I would get to see you again. And when you

kiss me, Garrett, I…I never want it to end."

I wrapped my arms around her waist, lifted her until our bare stomachs met then sealed her lips with mine.

***

"Were you a virgin before tonight?" she asked me as we lay so close our lips were almost in a perpetual kiss.

"Not really." My fingers traced up and down the side of her body from her thighs to her shoulder.

"Not really? Well, that's a complicated answer to a simple question?" She smiled. "Care to elaborate?"

I rolled over to my back. She snuggled close to me and rested her head on my chest. "In the eighth grade, I belonged to the science club. Keisha was the only girl on the team. One night we all went to her house to study for an upcoming competition. After a while, everyone went home except me. I wasn't in a rush to get home. Anyway, we kept studying. Then, out of the blue, she kissed me. When I asked her why she did it, she said she just wanted to know what it was like. So we kissed again. Then, somehow, we decided we wanted to find out what sex was like, so we did it. It was very mechanical. Two nerds performing a science experiment. We didn't even get completely undressed or turn out the lights."

Maddie chuckled a little on my chest and said, "That sounds pretty awful."

"Yeah it was. I don't think Keisha and I ever spoke again after that night." We both laughed. "What about you? Were you a virgin?"

"Yeah, but not from lack of trying. When I was 13, I was hospitalized for the umpteenth time. I thought I was going to die. I didn't want to die a virgin, so I started scoping out possible candidates right there in the children's ward. I settled on this 15-year-old named Charlie who had leukemia.

Well, I threw myself at him. I flirted, bought him gifts, went to his room constantly. Basically, I stalked him." Maddie paused.

"What happened?"

"We got to second base one night. But three days later…he died." Maddie grew silent. I stroked her back and stared at how the moonlight glistened over her platinum blonde curls. She was quiet for so long, I was afraid she had fallen asleep. I didn't want her to fall asleep. I wanted to keep talking to her.

"Maddie," I said trying to gently awaken her. "Why don't you ever mention your mother?"

"Because I don't remember her," she said with a yawn. "She died when I was a two. That's why my father flips out over anything that poses the slightest threat to my health. I'm all he has." Maddie propped her head up on her fist and stared at me. "Well, me and his politics. He's a senator, you know?" she added. "Why don't you mention your father?"

"He's in jail." Maddie winced as if the simple thought was painful.

"How long has he been in jail?"

"All my life, I just met him for the first time a little while ago."

"What did he do?"

"He…um…apparently he killed my grandfather."

Maddie gasped and she sat upright. "Oh my God. Oh my God, why?"

"I have no idea." I shrugged then went on to explain to her that so much of my life was a mystery.

"Garrett, we're gonna figure this out together. If they won't tell you the truth, well, I'll help you. I'm sure my dad has connections. We can look up the old court case, or find the lawyers, or even the judge. Whatever it takes. We're gonna find out what's going on." Maddie slammed her fist

into the bed as a sign of her determination, causing her breasts to jiggle. A smile formed on my lips partly because I loved how willing she was to help me and partly because I loved to watch her breasts bounce. She noticed my stare and covered her chest in embarrassment.

I sat up and unfolded her arms revealing her delicious womanly body. Then I lowered her to the bed and made love to her again.

***

Maddie awoke with a start.

"My phone. My phone's ringing. Don't you hear my phone ringing?" She jumped out of bed and searched for her phone. At first, I didn't hear a thing. I thought it was her imagination. Then I heard the faint ring. "Where's my phone?" she yelled frantically.

"In the living room on the coffee table next to the candy jar."

Maddie stopped tossing clothes in the air and looked at me.

"How do you know that?"

I pointed to my head and said, "Photographic memory." She smiled then took off running to the living room.

A few seconds later she returned and said, "It's for you." For me? I only gave one person Maddie's number. I snatched the phone.

"Eden, are you okay?"

## Chapter 12:
## Surreptitious Healer

"It's not Eden damn it! It's your mother and it's two o'clock in the morning. Where the hell are you?"

I sighed in relief that Eden was not in trouble. I looked over at the clock. Sure enough, it was 1:58. I shook the grogginess from my mind and tried to figure out what happened. After the second time we made love it was only 9:30. We must have fallen asleep. I smiled at the thought. I rarely slept that long on any given night. Thoughts of physical trauma and violence often haunted my dreams preventing a night of completely restful sleep. Now that Eden and I had separate bedrooms, I sometimes went to her room during the night and watched her sleep making sure she was safe and at peace while the same security and serenity eluded me.

"Sorry, Holly. We were…watching a movie and I guess we fell asleep." I swung my feet over the side of the bed and searched the tangled sheets for my boxer shorts.

"Don't 'Holly' me!" she yelled. I slipped on my shorts and sat on the edge of the bed trying to figure out why she would be so upset. "I am your mother and I've been worried sick. I was just about to call the police. I woke up Eden to ask her if she knew anything and she said you gave her this girl's phone number."

"Mother," I said trying to remain calm, "I don't see what the big deal is."

"You don't see what the big deal is? It's…it's a school night and you're…way past…curfew."

"Curfew?" I couldn't believe she was upset with me for staying out late after the countless times she never came home at all leaving me to care for an infant child. I felt the sudden urge to remind her of this.

"Curfew? I'm surprised you know what that word means. Which of your boyfriends taught it to you?" I immediately regretted the words as soon as they left my mouth. It was a hurtful thing to say. But, a part of me felt she deserved it. Where did she get the right to suddenly be concerned about my safety after so many years of neglect and abuse?

I glanced over at Maddie. She wore a look of shock and confusion on her face as she slipped on my shirt to cover her glorious nudity. I felt the need to apologize, not for my mother's sake, but for Maddie's. I didn't want her to think of me as some sort of callous monster.

"I'm sorry, mother." She didn't respond. I think I really hurt her this time. "Mother, are you there?"

"You…um…you have an appointment with Richard in the morning. I'll call the school…and let them know you won't be in." She hung up.

I closed the phone and set it on the night stand.

"Wow, Garrett, that was pretty harsh," Maddie said as she approached me and stroked my hair. I wrapped my legs around her and held her waist. "I think maybe I bring out the worst in you. First, you break a standing date with your sister, now you're getting into fights with your mother. Maybe I'm not so good for you. I feel like I'm taking you

away from your family." Maddie tilted her head down hiding her beautiful eyes from me.

"Are you kidding me? You're the best thing to ever happen to me." I lifted her chin and kissed her lips. "Eden and I are fine. We're spending the day together on Sunday. As for my mother...we have...an unusual relationship. I know what I said was cruel." Shamed by the guilt, I looked down. "Sometimes, I'm not a nice person, Maddie. I don't know what's wrong with me. I just hope that once you get to know me better, you don't regret –"

She silenced the thought with a kiss.

"I may never know everything that you've been through. But I do know that you're a wonderful person with a delicate and loving soul. I will never regret being with you."

Early the next morning, I eased myself out of bed, careful not to wake Maddie then padded off to the kitchen. I wanted to surprise her with a nice breakfast. I was a pretty good cook for a teenage boy. I had a lot of practice due to the countless times I had to cook for me and Eden. And in those days, I had a lot less with which to work. I remember having to stretch miniscule amounts of food for weeks. Somehow, I made it work.

Maddie's kitchen, however, overflowed with food. I finished making the pancakes, ham and cheese omelets, and breakfast potatoes just as she emerged from the bedroom.

"Oh my God it smells good in here," she said, rubbing the sleep from her eyes.

"I made you breakfast." I kissed the side of her head and handed her a glass of orange juice.

"That's so sweet, Garrett." Maddie took a sip of the juice then started arranging some prescription bottles on the counter. She opened one, shook out a couple of pills then swallowed them without even taking another sip of juice. I stared in awe as she repeated this process with bottle after bottle. "Please don't stare at me. I already feel like enough of a freak."

"That's not why I'm staring. I don't think you're a freak."

"You don't?"

"No, I think you're incredible. I can't imagine what your life has been like."

She smiled, "Really?"

"Yeah. Do you want to tell me what the pills do?"

"Okay," she said tucking an adorably messy curl behind her ear. "These four, I can take on an empty stomach. But these," she said pointing to a group she had separated off to the left, "I have to take with food. So, it's really great that you made breakfast for me. I usually just have a protein shake. Anyway, this one suppresses my immune system so that my body doesn't reject the heart, these two protect against infection since I have a weakened immune system, these two are for my blood pressure, this one is another anti-rejection medication, these three are kind of like vitamins that just try to build me up since the other medications kinda break me down." She paused to see if I was still listening.

"So you take nine pills every day?"

"Well, this month. Sometimes my doctor changes things up because something's not working or he wants to try something new."

"I can't believe you do this every day."

"It's better than the alternative," she said staring down at her feet.

I kissed her. I couldn't help it. I didn't want to imagine what my world would be like right now if she had died and I had never met her. I wanted to enjoy her, every part of her. Her touch, her smell, her taste.

"Do we have time to…you know…before school?" I asked lowering her to the floor.

"Definitely."

\*\*\*

I walked Maddie to school then dashed to my appointment with Richard. I entered the waiting room just as Eden stepped out of his office.

"Hey, Bug. Where's my hug?" I asked cheerfully. She didn't leap into my arms as usual. Instead, she pouted her lips and stared at me.

"You didn't come home last night."

"I know. I'm sorry."

"You've never done that before. I was scared."

"I didn't mean to scare you, Eden. I just…I-"

"Did you have sex?"

"What?" My voice resonated so loud and powerfully that Eden jumped back a little. I grabbed her elbow and pulled her into the hallway away from the shocked faces of the other patients in the waiting room. "Eden, where did you get an idea like that?"

"I asked Richard what he thought you were doing last night and that's what he said." Eden's eyes watered as she twisted her beret around in her hands. "Did I do something bad?"

"No, you didn't do anything wrong," I said hugging her as tears began to fall. "Don't cry, Bug. I didn't mean to yell at you." I forced myself to remain calm and speak in a soothing voice though every part of me wanted to strangle Richard for having such an inappropriate conversation with my little sister. "Do you want to go for lunch when I'm done with my appointment?"

Eden wiped her tears away as she said, "I can't. I'm going to school. I have a math test this afternoon. But we're still on for Sunday, right?" She said smiling broadly.

"Museum, lunch, and movie, right? Just the two of us, right?"

"Of course." I kissed her cheek and hugged her just as my mother entered the building.

"You ready to go, Eden?" My mother asked, avoiding eye contact with me.

Eden cocked her head to the side and said, "Aren't we gonna wait for Gary?"

"Garrett can apparently take care of himself." She grabbed Eden's hand, then looked into my eyes and added, "He doesn't need me."

My concern over Richard's conversations with Eden trumped my worry over my mother's words. By the time I stepped into Richard's office, my anger had returned stamping out any thoughts of Holly.

"Why the hell are you talking to my sister about sex?" I said slamming the door behind me.

"Good morning, Garrett. It's 9:23. You're late." Richard glanced at his watch pretending I didn't scare him, but I saw the beads of sweat forming on his forehead. I definitely frightened him.

"I asked you a question." I walked towards him and towered over his round body as he sat in his favorite wooden chair. He jolted out of his seat and made his way to his desk as he wiped his forehead with a handkerchief.

After he had the security of the desk between us he said, "What I discuss with Eden is protected by doctor patient privilege. I think you should just calm down and have a seat before I have to call your social worker. This behavior you're exhibiting is disturbing and…and I feel you may be a danger to your family. You don't want to go to another foster home, do you?"

Did he really think I was a danger? How could he possibly believe that after all I've done all my life to protect them? No, there was definitely another reason why he felt so

99

threatened by me all of the sudden.

I stared at the large wet circles forming under his armpits. So much heat radiated from his face his glasses had started to fog.

When I didn't move, he placed his hand over his phone. He was really going to make a phone call that would separate me from Eden. I couldn't let that happen. I took a deep breath and sat down determined to study this man as closely as he had studied me for the past decade. Something wasn't right with him. And if it had anything to do with my sister, he would regret the day he ever met me.

# Chapter 13:
# Brewing Storm

The appointment with Richard proved worthless as I spent the entire time studying his actions and facial expressions while providing sarcastic, succinct, or shrouded answers to his probing questions.

He wanted to know whether my disregard for my mother's rules last night was a sign of things to come. Would I turn into the typical withdrawn and unruly teenager?

"Is that what you would prefer, Richard?" I asked, answering his question with one of my own. "Would that make you more comfortable to know exactly where I fit? To label me with some sort of textbook diagnosis?"

"Why are you always so...," Richard paused as he searched for the right word. I decided to help him out.

"Caustic, argumentative, obstinate, recalcitrant?"

"I was going to say difficult or defensive, but yes, all those adjectives fit as well."

I stared into his eyes with a cold glare. I thought about the way he'd acted toward me just minutes ago and said, "I could ask the same question of you."

He ended the session.

*** 

As I walked home from Richard's office I noticed the

dull gray sky. It was mid November and we were due for a snowstorm anytime. If Grandma Jean were alive, she'd be able to immediately tell me whether to expect bad weather.

"Storms a comin'," she'd say. "Feel it in m' knees." Sure enough, later that day some sort of storm would pass through. I'd crawl into the rickety old rocking chair with her and wait out the rain, or snow, or hail, from the safety of her lap.

Right now, a storm brewed in my life. I felt the winds of change pressing against the floodgates of torrential emotions. But I felt powerless and blind. There was too much I couldn't control and even more I didn't know. Lately, I had just wanted to forget everything and lose myself in my feelings for Maddie, but the run-in with Richard reminded me that I couldn't. I had a family to protect.

When I got home, my mother's car was in the driveway, but the house seemed empty. The blinds were drawn and the lights were off. I walked toward the phone to call Maddie when I heard, "You must think I'm the worst mother ever." My mother sat on the couch with her back to me staring at a blank TV screen. I really didn't know what to say to such a remark. It wasn't a question, so I couldn't respond with a yes or no. Even if it was a question, a simple answer like that wouldn't have been appropriate.

I knew what she wanted me to say. She wanted me to forgive her for the foster homes, the hospital visits, the hunger pains. Did she want me to say that my life could have been worse and to thank her for not abandoning me completely? I didn't think I could do that.

"I know I've hurt you and disappointed you time and time again, but I am trying. Can't you see that?"

"Yeah, I –"

"I've been sober for two years, Garrett. We've moved out of those shady neighborhoods. I married a good guy who takes good care of us. What more do you want from me?"

"Nothing, moth–"

"I'm trying so hard to be strong like your father was, like he taught me to be, but it's so hard. You have no idea what my life has been like, Garrett."

"You're, right, mother. I don't know what you've been through. You've never told me." My mother grew quiet. I thought once again the conversation had ended at a pivotal moment. She would find some excuse not to delve into her mysterious past. But she didn't.

"My parents were rich, you know? I was rich, but I wasn't happy. My childhood was…" She paused and rested her head in her hands. I stood perfectly still afraid that if I even breathed I'd somehow make her snap out of her sudden urge to talk. "When I met your father, he was everything I needed. He took care of me. He listened to me. He loved me." She gestured for me to join her on the couch. "Greg was smart, strong, and noble. I had no idea a man could ever make me feel so special. When I lost him, I spent years trying to find that kind of love again, but I couldn't. No one could replace your father." My mother looked into my eyes and added, "You remind me so much of him sometimes that it scares me. Not because I don't want you to be like him. He's a great man. I'd love for you to turn out like him. It scares me because…I don't want to lose you too." My mother broke down into tears and I gathered her into my arms.

"You're not going to lose me, mother."

"When you didn't come home last night I didn't…I thought maybe I'd finally driven you away."

"I'm sorry. I didn't know." I had no idea my mother cared for me so much. She had always kept me at arm's length only showing affection on sporadic occasions, hugging and kissing me only when she felt guilty for some dangerous situation she'd thrust upon me. I wished we were

closer, but she kept herself so guarded never letting me past her emotional fortress.

My mother sat up, wiped her tears on the sleeves of her bathrobe then said, "I'm sorry I'm throwing all this on you. I don't want to burden you with my problems. I've already taken away so much of your childhood. You've spent your entire life worrying about me and Eden and taking care of us. You deserve to be a kid, which includes staying out all night and scaring your mother half to death." She smiled a little and slapped me playfully on the arm. "Just call next time, okay? Let me know where you are and that you're not dead or –"

"In jail?" I volunteered. She looked down and nodded. Holly and I had finally had a moment of connection. For the first time, I felt like we were mother and son having a normal afternoon conversation on the couch. I should have just let things be. But I couldn't. That burning desire in me to know the truth, to know my past and hers, just wouldn't go away. "Mom, was your childhood so bad because of your father? Is that why my father killed him?"

My mother folded her hands in her lap and stared at her thumbs as she said, "I knew one day you'd want to know the truth. I knew I wouldn't be able to keep it from you forever." She let out a long breath. "I promise I'll tell you anything and everything you want to know. I just...I...I need more time, baby. I'm sorry." She covered her mouth and ran out of the living room, leaving me alone and just as confused about my life as I'd always been.

I sat on the couch contemplating all the uncertainties of the relationships between me, my mother, my father, and my grandparents. I then began to wonder how Eden fit into all of it. Then I remembered what had gotten me so upset earlier that day. I had to tell my mother that I didn't think Eden and I should see Richard anymore. I never liked Richard an

extraordinary amount, and now his questionable behavior made him fall further out of my good graces. Why would he threaten me like that?

The only thing certain in my life was Maddie. I longed for the next time I could look into her eyes while holding her in my arms. I picked up the phone to call her when Eden burst through the front door in tears and ran to her room. Corbin entered a few seconds later with a perplexed look on his face.

I ran to her room and tried the door. Locked. "Eden, what's going on? Open the door!"

"Go away!" she yelled. She'd never spoken to me like that before.

"What's wrong with her?" I asked Corbin as he stepped next to me in the hallway.

Corbin rubbed his temple in a frustrated manner and said, "She heard me and Dashanka talking about an upcoming swimsuit layout we're doing and she wanted to be one of the models. When I told her that you and your mother probably wouldn't approve, she flipped out. She said that everyone treats her like a baby and that she's not a baby."

Now it was my turn to be confused. Eden never behaved like this. She used to be such a happy child. All of a sudden, she'd transformed. There had to be a reason.

"Maybe your mother can talk some sense into her," he added.

"My mother is in her room crying," I admitted guiltily. Her anxiety was my fault.

"Great." Corbin pinched the bridge of his nose with his thumb and forefinger. "You handle Eden, I'll comfort your mother."

After ten minutes of trying to get Eden to open her door, I gave up and went to my room. Seconds later Maddie called.

"I know this is probably not the correct protocol after last night. I mean, I'm probably supposed to wait some unwritten amount of time before I call you, but I couldn't. I just can't stop thinking about you."

Just the sound of her voice sent a shiver through my body that I guessed was love. It was a feeling I'd never experienced before and it made everything else in my life just melt away.

"I'm thinking about you too."

"Can you come over tonight?"

"I don't know if I should. My mother is still pretty upset about last night and I have to go to North Carolina in the morning to see my father."

"Oh." Even over the phone I could see the disappointment in her eyes. "What about tomorrow night?"

"It's probably going to be late when I get back. Plus, I don't know if I'll be very good company after spending an entire day in a prison."

Maddie paused then said, "Garrett, do you not want to see me anymore or something?" Her voice sounded small and weak like she wanted to cry.

"Of course, I want to see you. You have no idea how badly I want to hold you again." How could I make her understand how much I needed her? I couldn't let her think I didn't care. "How about we spend the day together on Sunday? Then maybe I could…spend the night and we can go to school together on Monday."

"Are you sure your mom won't mind?"

"She should be cooled off by then. Is it okay if I spend the night?"

"Definitely."

Even though we talked for two more hours, it didn't dawn on me until a split second after we hung up that I already had plans with Eden for Sunday. Eden had acted so strangely all day I didn't know how she would react if I canceled on her. But I also couldn't cancel on Maddie. I wanted her more than anything in the world. The only solution was for all three of us to go out together. That turned out to be a big mistake.

# Chapter 14:
# Sunday

Saturday morning I sat at the breakfast table wearing my Sunday best watching the clock tick. It was after eight o'clock and my mother still hadn't emerged from her bedroom. At this rate, we wouldn't arrive at the prison until after lunch. I poured myself another cup of coffee and searched the newspaper for an intriguing word to memorize. Nothing struck me. I would probably just end up choosing something at random from my thesaurus.

I looked at the clock again. A quarter till nine. Ten more minutes and I would go knock on her bedroom door. What could be keeping her? Did she forget? Or maybe, she'd changed her mind about making me go each week. I loosened my tie thinking that had to be it. I could have a Saturday free to spend with Maddie. Just thinking about surprising her and showing up at her apartment excited me, but then Corbin came and dashed those dreams.

"Just be careful," he said tossing me a set of keys. He grabbed his camera bag and another set of keys and headed for the door.

"What are you talking about? Be careful doing what?"

"Your mother is in no state to drive right now. You're gonna have to drive yourself to North Carolina."

"But I don't have a license."

"I know you can drive. I've seen you do it. Just be

careful."

I looked down at the key chain and said, "Wait a minute, you want me to take your convertible? Why can't I take my mom's car?"

"I need your mother's SUV today. I'm doing a shoot on location and I need the space for camera equipment."

"But what if I have an accident? Are you sure my mother can't take me?"

Corbin set down his bag and came over to the table. "Look, Garrett, your mother is really messed up right now. She had nightmares all night. She cries for hours on end. I really want her to take it easy today. I don't want her under any more stress. You're a smart kid. I trust you. Just do the speed limit and avoid the police." Corbin patted me on the back and headed toward the door again. "By the way, Eden's coming with me. I thought it might make her feel better. Hope you don't mind."

Seconds later Eden trotted into the living room carrying a tripod and two more camera bags.

"Those are expensive. Be careful with them, Bug," Corbin said.

Bug? Since when did *he* start calling her Bug?

\*\*\*

My father waited for me in front of the same table we'd sat at before. He'd already made his first move on the chess board and silently waited for me to take my turn. We played an entire game without speaking a word except for 'check' and 'checkmate'. Then halfway through the second game he said,

"I hope you used protection."

"What?" I knocked over a couple of pieces on the chess board and frantically tried to return them to their correct

positions.

"That's not where my bishop was. I thought you had a photographic memory."

"I do. You just distracted me. How do you-"

"Holly called me. You really scared her, you know?

"Yes, I know. I just don't see…why do you assume…it's none of your business."

"The hell it's not. I'm too young to be a grandfather." My father smiled playfully, but I was not in a playing mood. He had no right to make such assumptions and delve into my sex-life. "Check," he said.

"Check what?" I asked. My father raised an eyebrow and nodded to the board.

"Oh, right."

"Believe it or not, you weren't an accident," my father said at the start of the next game. "Holly thought if she got pregnant, her father would see how serious we were. She thought he would let us get married. I was young and foolish and in love. I just went along with her. Your mother can be very convincing when she wants to be." My father smiled then nodded to the board indicating that it was my turn. Suddenly, chess was the last thing on my mind.

"Is that why you killed him? Because he wouldn't let you get married?"

My father started breathing heavily. "Is that what she told you?" His words were low and controlled like he held back a tidal wave of anger. I have to admit, I was a little frightened.

"No, no she didn't tell me anything, actually. All I know is that you're in jail for the murder of her father." I looked at the chess board and made my next move, trying to seem relaxed and unfazed by my father's sudden mood change.

"That's all you need to know. I don't want her going

into detail with you about it." My father stood up from the table and said, "Memorize the board. We'll continue this next week."

I thought about Maddie the entire way home. The truth was we didn't use a condom. It hadn't even crossed my mind. What if she got pregnant? What would we do? What would I do? I can't have a child. I'm only 16. Was I really destined to repeat my father's life? I hadn't met Maddie's father, but something inside me knew he wouldn't like me. How could he? He's a wealthy senator. I'm a poor black kid with an incarcerated father. I've been in and out of foster homes all my life. I knew he wouldn't think I was good enough for his daughter.

When I got home, I called Maddie.

"We didn't use a condom," I said as soon as she answered the phone.

"And hello to you too," she said playfully.

"This is serious. What if you're pregnant?"

"Not possible."

"Why not?"

"A pregnancy would be devastating to my health. I wouldn't be able to take my medication, my body might reject the heart, I could die –"

"Which is exactly why we should have used protection. What were we thinking?"

"Garrett, would you relax? I wasn't finished. Knowing what a pregnancy might do to my body, my doctors put me on birth control as soon as I... became a woman. I have an implant. So, like I said, it's not possible." I breathed a sigh of relief. "We can have sex anytime we want, no problem. Ten times a day if you want. That's not to say I want it ten times a day, I was just...it's just a figure of speech. But, I mean, it's not like I *don't* want it. I mean if you want to...then I want to –" I loved the way she rambled when she got nervous. I

could imagine her face turning red and her lips becoming dry. She probably licked them after each sentence. I loved how I still made her nervous even after how intimate we'd been. I loved everything about her. Suddenly, I couldn't hold it in any longer.

"Maddie, I love you," I blurted.

She paused, as did my heart, but it started again when she said, "I love you, too."

\*\*\*

The next day, Eden burst into my room at six in the morning, jumped on my bed and said, "How about before we go to the museum we go to breakfast, or better yet, stay there. I'll go make you breakfast." She hopped off the bed and dashed out the door.

"Eden, you can't cook!" I called after her, remembering last month when she tried to make me an omelet. I tried to explain to her that omelets shouldn't be crunchy, but she was firmly convinced that throwing out the shell was wasteful.

"Why are we getting on the red line? Isn't the Smithsonian on the blue?" Eden asked as I held her hand and led her through the metro station.

"Yeah it is. We're just gonna make a quick detour."

"Farragut North?" she asked noticing where we were exiting the train. "Are we going to tour an embassy?"

"Not exactly. We're gonna pick someone up."

Eden stopped in her tracks and crossed her arms.

"Maddie. Maddie's coming isn't she? You said it was just gonna be us."

"I know I did, Bug, but I really want you to get to know her. She's really important to me."

Eden pouted all the way to Maddie's apartment.

"Eden, please be nice. I want her to see how great you

112

are," I said as we rode the elevator to Maddie's floor. "I thought you said you'd love her because I love her? What happened to that?" Eden shrugged and rolled her eyes.

Maddie opened the door looking absolutely radiant. She had straightened her hair and let it elegantly cascade to the middle of her back. She wore a tight deep blue top that accentuated her breasts and her tiny waist. The fact that I hadn't seen her in two days made me want her so badly that I forgot my sister's presence, swept Maddie up into my arms and kissed her without even a hello.

"Gross," Eden said as she walked past us into the apartment. "Why is your furniture so old? I thought you were rich. Why don't you buy some new stuff?"

I let go of Maddie and glared at Eden mortified that she would say something so impolite. Maddie walked over to the couch and put her hand on it. I thought sure her feelings would be hurt, but she took Eden's comment in stride saying, "I agree. It feels like I'm living in a museum sometimes." Maddie smiled then added, "Matter of fact, we can skip the Smithsonian today and I could just explain all my family heirlooms to you. There's probably just as much history in this room than in all the Smithsonians combined." I stepped up behind her, put my hands on her shoulders and kissed the top of her head. I loved how she tried to make light of Eden's blatant hostility. I laughed thinking that Eden would soon join in the levity, but I was wrong.

"Whatever," Eden said taking off her coat and tossing it over the couch. "Bathroom?"

"Third door on your left."

As soon as Eden was out of sight, I picked up Maddie and tossed her onto the couch. She giggled as I climbed on top of her and started kissing her passionately.

"Garrett, stop. She'll be back any minute."

"All I need is a minute," I teased as I kissed her neck

113

and inched my hands up under her shirt. She felt so soft and warm. I knew I needed to stop, but I couldn't.

"Garrett, Eden already seems pissed at me." Maddie sat up and pushed me away. "I want to make a good impression on her. If she catches us like this, there's no chance of that." I ran my fingers through my hair and tried to calm my desire. Sensing my frustration, she said, "Look, how about tonight I introduce you to the hot tub. And don't bring swim trunks." A sly sensuous smile formed on her lips.

"If you're trying not to arouse me right now, you're failing miserably." I kissed her so firmly she let out a soft moan. Then we heard the bathroom door open. Maddie hopped off the couch and started pulling down her top and flattening her hair.

"You ready to go, kiddo?" she said cheerfully when Eden entered the living room.

Eden looked back and forth from Maddie to me a couple of times before settling on me and saying, "You're wearing her lipstick." Then she grabbed her coat and headed to the door.

\*\*\*

"But I thought you wanted to go to a museum?" I asked as we walked rapidly toward the metro station.

"No, *you* wanted to go to a museum. You always want to go to a museum. I want to go to the mall."

I grabbed her arm and made her stop walking for a moment to let Maddie catch up. She was so little she had a hard time keeping up with Eden's fast pace.

"But there's this really interesting exhibit on oceans at the museum of Natural History that I thought you'd-"

"I said I want to go to the mall."

"The mall?" Maddie panted when she caught up.

"You're my kinda girl. Which mall do you want to go to?" Eden shrugged and looked off to the side.

"Eden, Maddie asked you a question."

"That's okay, Garrett. Why don't we just go to Pentagon City? Would you like that, Eden?"

Eden just shrugged.

\*\*\*

"So, I was thinking about what we can do for your birthday," Maddie said while feeding me a french fry as we ate lunch. After twenty minutes of Eden rejecting our suggestions of where to eat, we ended up in the mall food court. Maddie thought a nice greasy hamburger sounded great since she hadn't had one in almost a year.

"My birthday?" I said almost choking on the french fry. I was surprised she even knew my birthday was coming up let alone that she had planned something for it. It apparently shocked Eden as well since she looked up from her plate for the first time in ten minutes. Maddie and I decided to stop trying to appease her and to ignore her sulking. We were going to make the best of our time together.

"Yeah, your 17$^{th}$ birthday is like three weeks away. We have to start planning."

"I already have his birthday planned. I don't need your help," Eden said viciously. Maddie's smile faded. She picked up a french fry and carefully applied ketchup down the center of it. I thought it was adorable the way she had to put ketchup on each fry individually. I'd never seen anyone else do that.

"Eden, don't be rude." I said the words as politely as possible, but fury shot from my eyes. She knew I meant business. She huffed and stared off to the side. "Maybe this year we can include Maddie in our plans."

"I don't want to cause any problems, I mean, if you two already have something you do every year that's fine. It's just that my dad has this cabin at a ski resort in Pennsylvania

and I thought since December ninth is on a Saturday that we could get some friends together and go up there for the weekend or something."

"Skiing? Gary, don't ski." Eden crossed her arms and glared at Maddie.

Before I could verbally chastise Eden for the rudeness and incorrect grammar, Maddie said, "Well, maybe *Gary* wants to learn." Apparently she was growing tired of Eden's hostility.

"And maybe you just don't know him like I do." Eden stood up from the table and planted her fists in her sides. "You don't know anything about him. You don't know that he hates the smell of pickles or that his favorite movie is Little Man Tate. You don't know that he refuses to cut his hair because his grandmother told him that's what makes him strong. You don't know that sometimes when he can't sleep at night he does pushups until his arms burn." Tears started flowing down Eden's face. I reached out to embrace her but she swatted my arm away. Maddie just stared in shock as Eden's hysterical tirade began drawing the attention of all the food court customers.

"Eden, I –" Maddie began.

"No, you listen. I've known him all my life. And I'll be around long after you break his heart and toss him aside. He's the only person in the world that loves me and you're not taking him away from me." Eden turned and ran into the bathroom.

I paused for a moment trying to comprehend what just happened. Then I looked at Maddie's completely red face.

"Are you okay?" I asked as I stroked her back. She nodded yes then quickly shook her head no as she burst into tears.

"She hates me," she said between sobs with her head buried in my chest.

"Please don't cry, Maddie. She's just a kid. She doesn't know any better. She's normally not like this, I swear. Something's wrong. Something's really wrong."

# Chapter 15:
# A Wanting Heart

After such an emotionally draining afternoon, none of us wanted to ride a noisy train back home. Maddie called her driver and the three of us rode in complete silence to Corbin's townhouse in Virginia.

Eden stared out the window with her fist under her chin studying the roadway as if she'd never seen I-95 before. Maddie sat on the other side of me staring up at the ceiling of the car. I reached out and tried to hold Maddie's hand, but she slipped it away not wanting to upset Eden any further with overt signs of affection. I don't think she realized how alienated she made me feel. My sister ignored me and now my girlfriend didn't want me to touch her.

When we reached the house, Eden jumped out of the car and ran inside without saying a word. I sighed, turned to Maddie, and said, "I'm so sorry this didn't turn out exactly as I'd hoped."

"It's okay," Maddie said breezily. She tried to act as though the day hadn't been equally stressful for all of us, but the remnants of tears betrayed that sentiment.

"No, it's not. I'm going to talk to Eden and we're going to make it up to you. Actually, I can start making it up to you tonight." I smiled and reached out to caress her cheek, but she grabbed my hand, stiffened her neck and shook her head.

"Um, I'm kinda tired. I don't think I'll be able to hang

out with you guys tonight. Um, I'll see you in school tomorrow." What was she talking about? What did she mean 'you guys'? I was pretty sure the hot tub invitation was just for me. I stared at her in confusion. Her pleasant, vague expression didn't change. In fact, she actually shook my hand as if we'd just met.

"Okay...I'll see you in school I guess." I paused momentarily and looked into her eyes for some sort of explanation for her strange behavior. When I saw none, I slid out of the car trying to preserve any remnants of dignity I had.

"Okay, bye." Maddie gave a quick wave then closed the door.

As the car drove away, she didn't even look back. I couldn't breathe. It was about 20 degrees outside, but a stifling heat engulfed me. Not the familiar heat from anger. I think it was...fear. Fear that I'd lost her or that she didn't love me.

When I finally entered the house, Holly and Corbin were in the kitchen feeding each other orange slices. They both giggled as some of the juices slid down Corbin's cheek onto his bare chest. A queasy feeling washed over me as my mother leaned forward and licked it off. Suddenly, I felt empathy for Eden. Is this what Maddie and I looked like? Disgusting. No wonder she was so upset. All morning Maddie and I kissed and embraced every chance we got. Maddie feeding me french fries and planning my birthday had merely pushed her over the edge. How insensitive of me.

Corbin lifted my mother onto the counter top and started to untie her bathrobe. I covered my eyes and said, "Whoa, hey, I'm standing right here!"

"Oh, sorry, Garrett baby. We didn't see you." My mother hopped off the counter and tightened her bathrobe.

"You two are back early. What happened?" Corbin

119

asked as he wet a towel and wiped his chest.

"Don't ask. I don't think Eden likes Maddie very much."

"Eden likes everybody," my mother said. I thought I noticed a tinge of worry in her tone.

"You mean you took Maddie on what was supposed to be your special day with Eden?" Corbin chuckled a little as he slipped on a T-shirt. "That was dumb."

"Yeah, I realize now that it wasn't the wisest decision, but I really didn't expect such a meltdown from Eden. I mean she really got hysterical and caused a scene at lunch. Is that normal?"

"Welcome to the land of teenage girls," Corbin said as he took out two bottles of water from the fridge and tossed me one. "Trust me. I deal with temperamental young models all the time."

"I have to agree with Corbin," my mother said. "Eden is growing up and going through changes. Being a teenage girl is tough."

"But she's only 11."

"She'll be 12 in two months. Close enough," Corbin said. "I suggest you ignore her tantrums. She'll get over it. I bet she apologizes to you by the end of the day."

Maybe they were right. I guess I just really didn't understand girls. I certainly didn't understand why Maddie acted the way she did a few moments ago. Since I was having such a nice open dialogue with my mother and Corbin, I decided to see what they thought about the situation.

"She did what?" my mother asked after I explained Maddie's behavior in the car. She placed her hands on her hips in a defensive posture reminding me so much of Eden. They looked a lot alike, except Eden's hair was a few shades darker and our mother was a couple of inches shorter. They both had a delicate angelic quality that commanded the attention of everyone in the room.

"Maybe she doesn't like public displays of affection." Corbin volunteered.

"She didn't seem to have a problem with it this morning at the mall."

"Well, she sounds like a rich stuck-up snob to me. Maybe you shouldn't see her anymore." My mother stroked my hair as an attempt to soften the harsh sentiment of her words, but she couldn't hide her immediate dislike of Maddie.

"She *is* rich, but she's not stuck-up," I said pulling my mother's hand away from my hair. "She already planned a birthday weekend for me at a ski resort. Would she do that if she didn't really care about me?"

"What about her parents? Have you met her father?" my mother asked seriously as she crossed her arms.

"Her mother is dead and her father is out of town."

"Have you met any of her friends?"

I thought for a second. I wasn't even sure if Maddie had any friends. But I didn't see what that had to do with anything. What did it matter if I knew her friends or not? I'm sure I'd get to know them soon. If not, I didn't really care. All I needed was her.

"Don't scare him, Holly. I'm sure Eden's temper tantrum just threw her for a loop. Give her a call and talk to her," Corbin advised before leading my mother off to their bedroom.

*A star without light*
*My soul starved of affection*
*A glimmer gone*
*A life without direction*
*So much to give*

*With no one to take*
*A weakened heart*
*Frail to the point of break*

I sat in my room writing poetry waiting for Corbin's advice to take effect. Any second I expected Eden to knock on my door and apologize, but she didn't. I thought about making the first move, but then I thought she might need more time with her emotions.

My pride wouldn't let me call Maddie. She knew how I felt. She knew I loved her. Even though I wanted to call her and ask her if I did anything wrong, ask her how I could fix things between us, I just couldn't bring myself to do it. I'd rather be alone for the rest of my life than succumb to such a pathetic display of weakness. I still couldn't believe I'd actually cried in front of her.

After hours of sitting, waiting, ruminating and writing, the phone finally rang.

"I'm so sorry Garrett. You gotta let me explain." Maddie said. I didn't respond. "I couldn't let Leonard know about us."

"Leonard? Who's Leonard?"

"My driver. He would've told my dad."

"So, you don't want your father to know about me?" This explanation wasn't making me feel any better. "Are you ashamed of me?"

"No. God no, Garrett. My father is just…he's really over-protective I guess is the word. Especially when it comes to me. I want to *tell* him about you before…before he meets you or…hears about you. Can't you understand that?"

*Wanting hearts believe all*
*In search of an innermost desire*
*Ignoring reason exploring possibility*

*In search of what they most require*

I said I believed her although her words created a small fissure of doubt in my mind with regard to her true feelings.

That night, I ended up back in her bed. For a while, I forgot the day. I forgot Eden. I forget Maddie's reluctance to fully integrate me into her life. All I thought about was the intoxicating feeling of her body against mine. What happened the next morning, however, made a fissure of doubt evolve into an impassable chasm.

# Chapter 16:
# Morning Betrayal

"Oh, my God!" Maddie said bolting upright in bed.

"What is it? Are you okay?" I sat up and tried to stroke her back, but she hopped out of bed and frantically threw on her nightgown. "What time is it? Are we late for school?"

"Shh! My dad's home. You gotta hide," she whispered.

"What? Why?" I stood up and stretched not quite understanding why she was so upset.

"What do you mean 'why'? He can't meet you for the first time naked in my bed in the middle of the night!" Maddie ran around her room picking up my clothes then shoved them into my arms.

I looked at the clock. It wasn't exactly the middle of the night. I thought Maddie might be overreacting a bit. I wondered if Holly would care if I had a girl in my bed at six o'clock in the morning. Probably not. She definitely had done the same thing on several occasions. And she didn't mind me spending the night with Maddie as long as I told her beforehand. But then again, Holly wasn't what you would call a normal parent. I didn't know how "normal" families worked, but I guess I could understand how a father would be upset over a boy in his teenage daughter's room.

"Bathroom, no closet, no bed. Get under the bed," she said spinning around and pushing me.

I slid under the bed, with my clothes in hand just as I

heard a soft tapping on the door.

"Are you awake, Madison?" Senator McPhee called through the door.

Maddie jumped into bed, pulled the covers up and said, "Yes, Daddy."

"Good, I have exciting news to tell you," he said as he entered. "Are you feeling all right, sweetheart? You look flustered." The bed creaked and lowered nearly squishing me as he sat down on it. He must have been a large man. "Your pulse is racing. Have you been taking your meds?"

"Yes daddy."

"I knew I should have hired a nurse for you for the weekend. I can't believe I let you talk me into letting you stay here alone." Senator McPhee stood and walked to the bathroom. Good thing I didn't hide there.

"I'm fine, daddy."

"Here, drink this," he said, returning from the bathroom probably with a glass of water.

"Really, I'm fine…I just had a bad dream." She paused while she gulped down the water. "Why are you back so early? I wasn't expecting you until this afternoon."

"Like I said, I have exciting news to tell you. I couldn't wait."

"Okay, shoot." Maddie set her glass down on the night stand and adjusted herself in bed.

"After much consideration, I've decided to run for President."

"President? Of what?" she said after a pause.

"Of the country."

"This one?"

"Of course this one."

"Oh, okay," Maddie said.

"That's it? That's the only reaction I get out of you? This is big news!" The senator chuckled. "Well, maybe 16-

year-olds have more important things going on in their lives. So, what have you been up to this weekend?"

I thought this would be the perfect time for her to broach the subject of a boyfriend. Or, at least to mention that she'd met someone special, but she didn't. Instead she said, "Nothing. Um, I straightened my hair."

"I noticed. It looks great. Any particular reason? You only do that for special occasions. Are you trying to impress someone?"

"No, I just wanted something different." Why did she lie? She just told me she wanted to tell her father about me before he met me and now that she had the perfect opportunity, she chose to lie instead.

"Leonard says you went to the mall yesterday." The senator paused waiting for further explanation from his daughter.

"Uh-huh. I went to the mall with some…friends…from school."

"Well, that's great, sweetheart. It's good to see you finally making friends. But next time, you need to let me know who they are beforehand. From this point on, I need to run a background check on everyone you spend time with. I'm a presidential candidate now."

"The election is like two years away. You haven't even gotten the party nomination yet." Maddie whined.

"It doesn't matter. We are constantly going to be in the news. In fact, I have a press conference tomorrow and I want you to be there with me."

"Why should I be there? *You're* running for President not me." I could virtually see Maddie's big blue eyes sadden.

"You're my daughter and I would like to have your support. Plus, the press is going to be just as interested in my beautiful teenage daughter as they will be in me. My PR coordinator actually wants you to do some interviews soon.

He may be able to get you on MTV or something. Would you like that?"

"MTV? I hate MTV!"

The senator chuckled again. "Well, in any case, you are going to be very important to my campaign. That's why I can't have you around people that may damage our reputation. I'll probably have to take you out of school so you can join my campaign tour."

"But Daddy-"

"No 'buts', sweetheart. Now why don't you lie down for a few more minutes? I'm going to hop in the shower then I'll order in some breakfast. Do you want me to lay out your uniform?"

"No, Daddy, I can-"

"It's no problem, just relax." He went to her closet and shuffled through her clothes. *Good thing I didn't hide there either.* The senator placed her clothes on the bed, kissed her then left the room.

Maddie didn't say anything until she heard the water running in her father's bathroom.

"You can come out now."

I slipped out from under the bed and jumped into my jeans as quickly as possible. I needed to get out of there before I said something I regretted. Something to the effect that Maddie didn't think I was good enough to even come up in conversation with her father. Apparently, I was only good enough for sex. That would be fine for most teenage boys, but I wanted more. No, I needed more. I thought Maddie was the source of love and acceptance I'd been looking for, but I guess I was wrong.

"Garrett, please say something." Maddie stood up and tried to look into my eyes.

"I have nothing to say." I stuffed my underwear and my socks into my pockets as I stepped into my sneakers.

"I'm gonna tell him about us, I am," she pleaded as she wrapped her arms around my waist and kissed my chest. "I just have to wait for the right time. Now is not the right time. You heard him. He's running for President for Christ's sake. I couldn't let him know that-"

"That what?" I unwrapped her arms and held her wrists. "That you're in love with a black boy? Or that my father's a murderer? Or that my mother is a former drug addict and alcoholic? Or that I've stabbed a man?" Her eyes watered. "Trust me, Maddie, I completely understand. I knew when I met you I wasn't good enough for you."

"Garrett, don't say that. I –" Maddie stopped abruptly as the water in her father's room stopped running.

"It's been fun, but, this just isn't going to work," I said in a controlled whisper, trying to hold back what I really felt. I kissed her forehead, slipped on my T-shirt, then headed for the door.

"Th-that's it? It's over?" I didn't respond. As I made my way down the hallway, as quietly as possible, I heard her burst into inconsolable tears. My heart yearned to run back, hold her in my arms and tell her we could work it out, but my mind told me we couldn't.

# Chapter 17:
## Despair

Rain and sleet fell upon the windshield of Corbin's car as I made my way home that morning. I focused on the road before me and drove as carefully as possible. The last thing I needed was to crash Corbin's car. Then, for a brief moment, a dark thought clouded my mind. Maybe a car accident *is* what I needed. One jerk of the wheel over the side of a bridge and this gnawing pain in my heart would disappear. Eden's face flashed in my mind's eye and I quickly vanquished that thought.

What the hell is the matter with me? Maddie's just a girl. Why am I making this into such a big deal? I could get over her. I could find someone else. I would be fine. The only problem was I didn't want anyone else. And no matter how hard I concentrated on controlling my emotions. I wasn't fine and I didn't know if I would ever be.

"What are you doing here? I told you to keep the car for the day," Corbin said as he ate cereal with Eden and my mother at the breakfast table.

"Leave me alone," I snapped. I threw the keys at him with a little more force than I intended and knocked over a glass of milk. It crashed to the floor causing everyone to stare at me in dismay.

"Garrett, you apologize to Corbin right now!" my mother yelled while Corbin scrambled to clean up the mess. I

ignored them and headed to my room.

"It's okay, Holly. He's obviously upset over something," Corbin said.

"I bet it has something to do with that stupid girl," Eden said disdainfully.

Corbin took Eden to school so she wouldn't have to ride the metro by herself. My mother spent the next two hours trying to get me to talk and open up to her, but I couldn't.

"Garrett, baby, please tell me what happened. I'm your mother. I want to help you," she said through the door.

"Just go away. You won't understand." She'd never understand my pain. She'd probably side more with Maddie in this situation considering the same thing kind of happened with her father and my father. She'd probably think it best that Maddie and I ended our relationship. She wouldn't want history repeating itself.

I lay in my bed staring at the ceiling trying to purge thoughts of Maddie from my mind, but to no avail. I tried to write my feelings, but found only a blank page confronted me. I tried sleeping, but sleep avoided me.

What felt like moments after I laid down, Eden knocked on my door. Reluctantly, I let her in.

"Mom says you haven't eaten all day," she said handing me a sandwich on a plate.

"Thanks," I mumbled before placing it on the dresser and plopping back down on the bed.

"I went to your teachers today. You have tests in Calculus and English tomorrow, and your history teacher says you have to turn in some project before Thanksgiving break.

"Thanks." I returned to my familiar position of staring at the ceiling.

"I wrote it down for you."

"I got it, thanks." The finality of my tone should have made her leave, but it didn't. She continued to stand at the foot of my bed and stare at me.

"You missed a Chemistry quiz today. Your teacher said he'd let you make it up if you bring in a doctor's note and Richard said he'd write you one if you come see him this week."

"When did you talk to Richard?" I sat upright in the bed.

"I didn't. Mom called him when you wouldn't come out of your room. He really wants to see you."

"Well, I don't want to see him and I don't think you should either." Eden grew quiet. I stared into her eyes looking for some sort of reaction. I thought her eyes would reveal the truth behind her interactions with Richard, but they didn't. They remained blank, cold, and expressionless. Come to think of it, her eyes were like that a lot lately. I remember a time when Eden's eyes sparkled adding light and joy whenever she entered the room, but now, that formerly innate happiness had disappeared.

"I talked to her," she said after a few minutes. I knew she meant Maddie. I lay back down in the bed unresponsive. "I barely understood a word she said she was crying so hard." Eden sat on the edge of my bed. "I'm sorry I was such a brat yesterday. I didn't want you to break up with her. I just…I just wanted…I don't know what I wanted." She put her face in her hands.

"I didn't break up with her because of you. It's complicated."

"Do you want to talk about it?" she asked hopefully. She turned away when I didn't respond.

Eden continued sitting at the foot of my bed staring off into space for about an hour. Then she quietly left my room.

131

I went to school the next day, not because I wanted to, but because my mother threatened to have Richard come to the house. I didn't want that man in my home.

I knew Maddie wouldn't be at school. I remember her father saying he had a press conference on Tuesday. She might not be coming back to Barton Arms at all if her father decided to take her on the road. I may never see her again. Ironically, that thought comforted me. Yes, I knew I loved her, but a part of me was embarrassed for letting myself get so close to her only to be rejected. If I never saw her again, maybe I could pretend like none of it ever happened.

That turned out to be harder than I thought.

During lunch, Eden and I sat in the cafeteria eating silently. Well, actually, I ate. Eden said she didn't have much of an appetite so she just stared at her plate of food.

"Are you all right, Bug?" I asked when I noticed she hadn't touched her food.

She nodded but didn't start eating. "You're not upset about Maddie are you? I told you it wasn't your fault. We broke up because...because she doesn't love me," I said realizing the awful truth. Even though she said she loved me, she really didn't. If she did, she'd be able to accept me into her life.

I wanted the conversation about Maddie to end there, but then all the TV monitors in the cafeteria clicked on and I saw Bartholomew McPhee standing at a podium. He started talking about his decision to help lead this country to greatness by running for President while Maddie stood by his side doing her best to look confident and comfortable. I knew she must have been extremely nervous though. She kept licking her lips and gently swayed from side to side. One of Senator McPhee's advisors actually tapped her on the shoulder to make her stop.

When the press conference ended, Barton Arms

students cheered riotously.

"Good job landing the next first daughter," Troy Stanton said jokingly while patting me on the back. I don't know how he knew about me and Maddie. I never told anyone and I was pretty positive Maddie hadn't either. But then again, he could have just been one of the dozen kids who saw us kiss on the front steps of the building a while ago. Rumors started and traveled fast in high school. I failed to realize that as I grabbed his wrist, twisted it around his back and slammed his face into the table. Unlike public schools where a crowd would have instantly gathered and cheered on a fight, Barton Arms students just stopped and stared at me. A few started whispering and pointing as if they knew something about my past. I felt like a pariah as I let go of my history classmate's arm and fled the cafeteria.

"Where are you going?" Eden asked as she caught up with me outside of school.

"Home."

"Well, I wanna go with you."

"Go back to school, Eden."

"But, you need me."

"I don't need anyone," I snapped as I quickened my pace toward the metro station.

I didn't go straight home. Somehow I ended up at Richard's office. Even though logically I knew he had nothing to do with what was going on with Maddie and me, for some reason my anger focused on him. Maybe it was a coping mechanism. I just needed someone to blame.

"You can't go in there," the receptionist Mrs. Swisher said as I stormed past her desk and straight into Richard's office.

He looked up abruptly when I entered the room. "Garrett, what are you doing here?" He quickly shuffled some papers around trying to cover up something.

I looked at the mess on his desk and noticed pictures scattered about. I looked more closely.

"Why are you looking at pictures of my sister?" I yelled. He didn't have a chance to respond. The last thing I remember is leaping across his desk and punching him in the face.

When I came to, I sat handcuffed in the waiting room.

"Do you want to press charges?" I heard someone say. I looked up and saw a police officer talking to Richard.

Richard pulled a bloody cloth away from his mouth and said, "No. He's my patient. He needs a hospital not a jail."

"Well, we can keep him in custody until you get the paperwork ready to have him committed."

Richard dabbed his lip with the cloth. He didn't respond to the officer immediately. He seemed pensive. Oh my God, he was actually contemplating putting me in a mental institution. If he had me committed, no one would believe me when I accused him of inappropriate behavior with Eden. I wanted to scream. I wanted to tell that police officer that Richard should be the one to be arrested, but I had to be extremely careful of how I proceeded. Richard held my future in his fat, grubby hands.

"No," he said finally. "I don't want to separate him from his sister. I don't think she could handle that. He's emotionally unstable, but I don't think he's a real threat."

Richard had no idea how much he underestimated me.

When I got home, I tried to watch some TV, but it didn't help. Every station seemed riveted on the fact that Bartholomew McPhee was running for president. Over and over the newscasters harped on the fact that he had lost his wife in a car accident 16 years ago and that his only daughter suffered from a debilitating heart disease resulting in a transplant two years ago. The way they focused on the tragedies in his life, I thought sure he would be elected just

on sympathy alone.

"What are you doing home?" my mother asked when she came downstairs as I flipped through channels searching for anything that didn't have 'McPhee' scrawled across it.

I shrugged and continued pressing buttons on the remote. Holly stared at me strangely. She probably thought it odd not only that I was home in the middle of the day, but that I was watching TV. I rarely watched TV, but I wasn't interested in doing the things I normally enjoyed.

"What time is it?" she asked looking at her watch.

"You have the watch. Why don't you tell me?"

My mother looked at her watch again then glanced at the door.

"Why don't you take my car and go pick up Eden from school?"

"I just got here. Why don't you pick her up?" My mother looked at her watch again. "Are you expecting someone? Are you trying to get rid of me?" I asked.

Holly sighed and said, "Someone is coming…and I think it might be best if you're not here."

I clicked off the television and looked at my mother. My curiosity had been piqued. Who was coming that made my mother so nervous? Why was I suddenly not wanted in my own house?

When the doorbell rang, my mother froze with fear giving me time to bolt off the couch and beat her to the door. I wish I hadn't. I wish she would've warned me that the Devil himself had been invited over.

# Chapter 18:
## The Devil Incarnate

"Long time no see, little buddy," Joel said as he dropped his cigarette on the front step and snubbed it out with his foot. He said it sarcastically. It had to be sarcastically. We were never buddies. I remember him telling my mother one time that he thought I was crazy and that I would end up killing him in his sleep. He wanted her to send me back to foster care, but my mother wouldn't do it. That's ultimately why they broke up the second time. Looking back now, I should've done it. I should have killed him in his sleep.

The lit cigarette moved in slow motion from his fingers to the ground as I stared at it having lost all ability to speak. My chest ached, no, it burned. And that burning grew with each second he stood in front of me. Why was he at my door? I'd hoped to never see him again.

For a moment, I felt like I had transformed back into that powerless child that let him burn me over and over. His face looked exactly the same as it did that night. Even though now I could probably take him out with one punch, a latent fear of him resided in me. But that fear quickly morphed into anger. A fire-like anger that could only be doused by giving back to him the pain he had inflicted on me. I felt my body lean toward his to seek my revenge when my mother grabbed my arm and said, "Come in and have a seat, Joel," as she pulled me into the kitchen.

"Garrett, let me explain," she began. I only half listened to what she had to say. I couldn't take my eyes off Joel in my living room. He looked almost exactly the same. Even with his coat on, I could still see some of the tattoos on his neck and hands. He was still bald by choice making him look like one of those Neo-Nazi's or skinheads. He wasn't as tall as I remembered, probably because I had grown so much in the five years since I'd last seen him. "When I asked Joel to relinquish his parental rights, he decided he wanted to be a part of Eden's life and sued for joint custody. We're in negotiations right now and I'm considering letting him take Eden for Thanksgiving."

This caught my attention. "He's not taking my sister anywhere." My jaw tightened and my hands clenched into fists.

"Calm down, Garrett. This is why I didn't tell you what was going on. I didn't want to upset you." Joel took his coat off, slung it on the back of the couch and made himself comfortable further incensing me. How dare he come into my home as if nothing happened? As if he hadn't tortured me.

No, I wouldn't calm down. I didn't want to calm down. This day had been long coming, but it was finally here. Today Joel would pay for what he did.

"Damn right I'm upset! I don't want him anywhere near Eden." Joel heard this remark. He turned around and smiled at me. I lunged forward but my mother squeezed my arm and pulled me further into the kitchen where Joel wouldn't be in my line of sight.

"Garrett, he's her father. He has a right to see her if he wants to."

Just then Corbin came downstairs. "Hello, Mr. Thompson," he said to Joel. I yanked my arm free of my mother's grasp and stormed back toward the living room.

Joel stood up and shook hands with my stepfather.

"Wait a minute. Even Corbin knew about this?"

"Baby, just calm down. We're trying to figure out what's best for our family."

"What's best for our family is if he stays the hell away from it," I yelled as I pointed to the evil monstrosity that had just reentered our lives. Both Corbin and Joel looked at me. Corbin with concern, Joel with disdain. Then Joel smiled again while taking a cigarette out of his pocket.

When he reached for his lighter, Corbin said, "There's no smoking in here, Mr. Thompson." Joel ignored him and stared directly at me as he flicked on his lighter.

Corbin ran his fingers through his recently highlighted hair as his faced flushed with embarrassment that he had been so directly defied, but there was nothing he could do. Even if Joel didn't have three inches and 50 pounds on him, Corbin was just not the fighting type. Corbin looked more appropriate picking out a wine for dinner or helping my mother decide which necklace brought out her eyes. That's not to say I didn't respect Corbin. He treated my mother well and he provided for us in a way that no other man had. But he wasn't a protector. That, once again, was my job.

"You heard him, Joel. No smoking," I said as I stepped out of the kitchen into the living area and folded my arms with intimidation. Only the couch separated us. And with one quick move, I could grab him. Uncertainty flashed in Joel's eyes. I could tell he didn't want to push me too far, but he also didn't want to back down. We stared at each other for what seemed like an eternity.

Finally, Joel flicked off the lighter and said, "Look, I don't want any problems. I just think I should be allowed to see my daughter." Joel returned the lighter to his pocket, but kept the cigarette between his fingers.

"That's what we're gonna try to figure out, Joel," my

mother said as she stood next to me and rubbed my back trying to calm me. "We're going to come up with something that's fair."

"What's fair is if I get half the money. She has half my genes. I think I deserve half her money."

"What money?" Corbin and Holly said almost in unison.

"All that money she's making posing in them pictures. I seen her just the other day in some magazine."

So all he wanted was money. He didn't care about Eden in the least. Of course I knew that. Joel wasn't physically capable of caring about anyone. I had no idea what my mother ever saw in him.

I glared at Corbin. I knew no good would come from Eden becoming a model. Having her picture plastered in magazines only brought her cretin of a father back into her life.

The shock of Joel's callousness and greed left my mother and Corbin momentarily speechless as he added, "I got me a lawyer and he says I'm entitled to the money."

"Mr. Thompson, there is no money. She just did a favor for me and posed for a couple of layouts," Corbin said still standing in the exact same place he had when he entered the living room. He had a hard time hiding his obvious fear of Joel.

"Well, then I'll take her someplace where she can make some real money. My lawyer says I'm entitled to that too."

"You're not getting anything, Joel, so just get the hell out!" I yelled.

"Goddamn it, Garrett, calm down and let me handle things for once. I'm the parent and you're the child. I can take care of it," my mother said obviously frustrated. It was a

tense situation. I could feel everyone's anxiety rising. I knew I should have walked away, but if I did, I knew nothing would happen. Or worse, Eden would end up with Joel. Even a little time alone with that man was too much for me to imagine. My mind flashed to all the things Joel could possible do to exploit my sister and try to make money off of her. I wouldn't let that happen.

I turned to my mother and ignoring my better judgment, I said, "Oh, so you suddenly want to be a parent, Holly? Why don't you take a look at what happened the last time you 'handled things'?" I ripped open my shirt and exposed my scars. I don't know what made me do it then. Maybe I wanted to show just what sort of a monster Joel was. There was no way my mother would let Eden go with him if she knew what he had done to me.

Or maybe I was just hurting so bad inside that I wanted someone else to share my despair. My poor mother was an easy target.

"Oh dear God," my mother gasped as she hid her face in her hands.

"Don't hide from it, Holly. Look at what he did to me. Look at what you let happen!"

Corbin came over and embraced my mother as she started crying. "Who did this to you?" he asked.

"Why don't you ask him?" I responded, indicating Joel.

"What?" Joel said feigning innocence. "You can't prove that. Your psycho kid is just trying to distract you from the fact that I have rights. My lawyer says I have a shot at getting full custody once I show what a head case her brother is and what a slut her mother is."

I couldn't hold back any longer. My mother and I had problems, but no one called her a slut. And as for him getting custody of Eden, well, he would die right now at my hands before I'd let that happen. With that I leaped over the couch and tackled him getting into my third fight in one day. Joel howled in pain as he fell backwards over the coffee table and his head slammed into the edge of it. He rebounded by grabbing my collar then slamming his fist into the side of my face.

My mother begged us to stop as we began rolling around the floor, but this fight had been five years overdue and I knew it wouldn't stop until one of us was dead.

I grabbed Joel's ear and banged his head into the floor repeatedly. When my hand lost its grip on his blood soaked ear, he took the opportunity to kick me in the stomach and send me reeling backwards. He scrambled to his feet, jumped on top of me and continued his assault on my face.

He was beating me unconscious. I felt myself slipping away. I looked over and saw my mother crying and heard her yelling at the top of her lungs. My eyes then searched for Corbin, but he was nowhere to be found. If I died, who would protect her?

My mother found a broom and started hitting Joel in the back with it, but he ignored her like she was some sort of inconsequential fly and continued to beat me.

I gathered the last bit of strength I had, reached through Joel's arms and gripped his neck. He tried to scratch my hands away, but my fingers were securely locked around his windpipe squeezing the life out of him. His eyes bulged as he gasped for air.

A sudden silence fell upon the room. A stark contrast to the sounds of screams and hitting that prevailed just seconds before. Now all I could hear was the sound of Joel choking.

My mother dropped the broom. "Garrett don't," she said with an eerie calmness. She knew what I wanted to do. She saw it in my eyes. "Don't do this, baby. Let him go." But I couldn't. I couldn't let him go. If I let him go, that would

141

mean I forgave him for what he did to me. I still remember his eyes the day he took that cigarette and used me for a human ashtray. Anyone that would do that to a child deserved this.

I had just resolved in my mind to kill him right then and there when, with a final burst of energy, Joel reached into his pocket and pulled out some silver object. A flood of pain in my side caused my grip around his neck to loosen.

My mother let out a scream so filled with horror and pain that at first I thought something had happened to her. She knelt beside me and placed my head in her lap just as Joel lifted a knife drenched with blood into the air. I wondered whose blood was on that knife. My mother's hysterics made me think it was hers, but that wasn't possible. She had been standing behind him.

"Drop it, Joel," Corbin said as he stood over him holding a gun. Joel dropped the knife and backed away.

When did Corbin get a gun? And why didn't I know about it? I wondered what other things went on in this house that had escaped my attention. I had been so wrapped up in Maddie that I probably hadn't noticed a lot of things.

"I didn't mean to hurt him. It was self defense. He was gonna kill me. You saw it. He was gonna kill me. That kid is a psycho." Joel stood up slowly while coughing and rubbing his neck. He didn't take his eyes off of the gun pointed at his face.

Corbin's hand shook as he told Joel to sit in the kitchen and not move until the police arrived.

I tried to stand, but my mother told me to lie down until the ambulance came. Ambulance? Why would I need an ambulance? Then I remembered the pain in my side. I looked down and saw the blood gushing out.

## Chapter 19:
## Sisterly Love

"I feel like I'm ruining your life," Eden said as she stood in the doorway of my bedroom. I blinked away the grogginess and pushed myself up into a sitting position ignoring the pain. Even with the multitude of pain killers, I still felt like my side was ripping open. The blade hadn't hit any major organs so the doctors just stitched me up and sent me home. They were more concerned about the contusions on my face and head and the concussion I suffered than the stab wound itself. The first night home from the hospital, my mother stayed in my room waking me up every two hours to make sure I didn't slip into a coma. I told her this wasn't necessary. If the doctors sent me home I must be fine, but she refused to leave my side.

I'd been in bed ever since the incident with Joel and only ventured out for the Thanksgiving dinner my mother and Corbin had prepared. It was a somber occasion filled with guilt and long silences.

"What are you talking about?" I asked as Eden came over to the bed and checked my bandage.

"Do you want me to change it for you? Cause I can. Do you want some water or something? Are you hungry? I think there's some leftover turkey."

"That's okay. I'm fine."

Eden sat next to me on the bed. "I feel like this is my fault and I want to make it better."

"Eden, it's not your fault. Don't blame yourself." I pulled her to me and hugged her as she started crying.

"First, I chase away Maddie, the only girl you've ever loved. Then my father tries to kill you. You must hate me, right? You hate me, don't you?"

"I could never hate you. I love you more than anything in the world. Do you believe that?" She nodded while still wetting my t-shirt with tears.

"But you still love Maddie, too?" she asked as she pushed away a little and looked into my eyes. I sighed and struggled to find the right words to say. It had been less than a week since I last spoke to Maddie, but it felt like a lifetime ago. Our worlds were so far apart nothing was capable of bridging them together.

At first I avoided any mention of her or her father's name in the news, but lately, for lack of anything else to do, I had become obsessed with following the campaign trail. I knew every scheduled TV appearance and interview for Senator McPhee for the next two months. I didn't have any pictures of Maddie, so I looked forward to every opportunity to possibly see her face. It was pathetic, I know. And I hated myself for being so in love with her. For as long as I could remember, I'd tried my best to control my life, to protect myself and my family from any kind of pain. But I couldn't control this pain.

"Yeah, I still love her," I admitted guiltily. "But she doesn't love me. You had nothing to do with us breaking up."

"Well, I'm gonna get you back together. I'm gonna fix it. I am." Eden wiped the tears away from her eyes with new found determination. A sparkle returned to her eyes that I hadn't seen for weeks. I didn't feel like breaking her spirit and telling her it wasn't possible.

Under the circumstances, my father allowed me to miss a visitation with him the next Saturday. He said we'd pick up our game of chess in a few weeks. I was fine with that. I didn't want to see anyone. I didn't even want to leave the house. Both my mother and Eden were afraid that I was falling into a depression. They did whatever they could to cheer me up, but nothing worked. I stayed in bed staring at the television like a vegetable refusing to write poetry or study the dictionary like I used to.

I even refused to go to school. I didn't want to have to explain where all the bruises on my face came from. Eden brought my work home to me every day and I was able to stay on task.

She also got in the habit of hanging out in my room for hours after school. I didn't mind. I liked having her around, but I kind of felt I was a bad influence on her. I thought she should be out living her life instead of watching me wallow in self pity.

"Why don't you go to the studio with Corbin? I'm sure he could use your help with something," I suggested one afternoon. Eden shrugged and continued to stare at the TV.

"Richard doesn't think it's a good idea that I spend so much time with Corbin," she said after a moment.

"What does Richard have to do with any of this?" I asked, sitting up in bed a little. He obviously hadn't learned anything from the physical altercation we'd had.

Eden didn't respond at first. She dipped her apple slice into the bowl of purple dyed Cool Whip that sat in her lap. When she was little, she always wanted me to dye food to her favorite color purple before she would eat it. She thought it made the food prettier, thus more edible. She

hadn't done it in years, but recently I'd noticed that many of the concoctions she brought me to eat or drink had a purple tinge to them.

Eden sucked the Cool Whip off the apple slice then said, "After you got stabbed, I was so depressed that I started seeing Richard more often. Just about every day. I needed someone to talk to."

"Why didn't you talk to me or mother?"

"You're recovering. I didn't want to bother you. And mom…well, she's too concerned about you to care about what's happening to me."

"That's not true."

Eden shrugged. "Anyway, Richard thinks I need more friends my own age and that all the time I've been spending with models and stuff isn't good for my self-image. He doesn't want me to grow up too fast. He thinks that's part of *your* problem. You never got to be a kid."

"My problem? What does he know about my problems? He *is* my problem." I lay down in the bed at stared up at the ceiling. Where did he get off telling my sister how to live her life? He had no clue what was best for her. I'm the one that knew what she needed and how to make her feel better. "Have you written any poems recently?" I asked.

"No," she replied simply.

"Well, why don't you go do that?"

"I'd rather just stay here with you," she said. Then she looked at me with her big brown-green eyes. Her eyes were pleading. Pleading for what, I couldn't tell.

I began to lose track of time. One day melded into the next with complete monotony. My bruises looked better, but were still noticeable. The stab wound only hurt to the touch. It wasn't my physical ailments that kept me in bed. It was something else.

"Okay, get up," Eden commanded one morning as she

drew the blinds allowing the obnoxious sun to pour in. "Take a shower and put this on," she said as she plopped some clothes on the bed.

"What? Why?" I asked. I sat up in bed and tried to avert my eyes from the sun.

"It's your birthday and I have a big day planned."

I sighed. "Eden, I appreciate the gesture, but I'm really not up to it." I lay back down in the bed and said, "Besides, there's an interview on C-SPAN that I really want to see today."

Eden stared at me blankly for a moment visibly planning her next move, trying to think of something to say that would get me out of bed, something different than all the things she'd said in the past three weeks that didn't work. Apparently, she couldn't think of anything; instead, her lip began to quiver and a second later she burst into tears.

I jumped out of bed and held her in my arms. I hated seeing my sister cry.

"Nothing's right. Everything's wrong," she said through the tears. "I just want to take my big brother out for his birthday. Please, Garrett. It would make me so happy. I'm so unhappy, Garrett. Don't you want me to be happy?"

"Okay, Okay, Eden. We can go. I'm going to the shower right now."

She calmed down a little and wiped away the tears with her fingertips.

"Can I brush your hair like I used to?" she said recovering from her outburst with little gasps for air.

"Sure," I said. A small smile formed on her lips.

"You got him out," my mother said excitedly to Eden as I entered the living room. I noticed a strange smell. I looked down and saw the brand new carpet. It went without saying why it had been installed. After two weeks of my

mother scrubbing the carpet, the blood stains from the fight with Joel hadn't completely come out. She must have just given up and had it replaced.

My mother crossed the room and hugged me tightly burying her face in my chest. As I held her in my arms, we shared a special moment of understanding. Deep down I knew she loved me and she wouldn't purposely let harm come to me. She was weak and had honestly done the best she could in the circumstances she was given. I still had a mental vision of her beating Joel with a broom stick in my defense and sitting by my bedside all night watching me sleep. Only a mother who cared would do that.

"I promise I will never let you get hurt again," she said as she pulled away with tears in her eyes. "No matter what I have to do. I promise, Garrett. I swear it." Something about the determination in her green eyes, the eyes that were exactly like mine, made me believe her this time.

The special day Eden planned for me began with breakfast at the Barnside Diner. It was a 50s style greasy spoon near the neighborhood where we used to live. It held a lot of memories for me and Eden. On weekends we had gone there to eat breakfast and to avoid my mother's alcohol induced rages or drug induced stupors. We sometimes stayed there for hours playing our word game or writing poetry. The wait staff knew us by name and often gave us extra food. Though we never said anything explicitly, I think they assumed we had a difficult home life and tried to take care of us.

As soon as we entered the door, Anabel and Darlene scrambled across the diner and tackled us with hugs.

"Mi chula, mi chulo, it's so good to see you," Anabel said in her thick Spanish accent. She was a cute little El Salvadorian woman in her 20s who had been working at the Barnside since she was 15. This diner was her home, and for a long time Eden and I were her little brother and sister.

"My God, you're huge," Darlene said to me. "And gorgeous as all get out. I swear if I were 30 years younger, you'd be in trouble." Darlene then inspected my face for a moment. I could tell she noticed the bruises as a motherly expression befell her. She chose not to comment on them, however, and just gently rubbed my cheek as she said, "I'm glad you're here."

"You two sit at the counter and order anything you want. It's on me," Anabel said as she took Eden's hand and led us to our favorite spot.

"Hey, Eddie, you owe me 20 bucks. I told you they would come," Darlene yelled to the kitchen as she adjusted her massive bun of gray hair.

Eddie poked his head out of the kitchen. "Welcome back guys. Happy birthday, Garrett," he said then quickly went back to filling his orders.

Eden and I spent the next two hours playing the word game with Anabel and Darlene. Some of the other customers even jumped in from time to time. It was the most fun I'd had in a long time.

Suddenly a middle aged woman sitting in one of the booths said, "Wait a minute, this is you isn't it?" as she stood and slapped a magazine down in front of my sister.

Anabel snapped it up and took a look. "Oh my God, it is you!" she exclaimed. "Why didn't you tell us you were a Gap model?"

"I don't really want to talk about it," Eden said meekly as she started in on her french toast again even though it had to be cold by then.

"But why not? You look beautiful," Anabel prodded.

"Hey, if she doesn't want to talk about it, she doesn't want to talk about it," Darlene said in an authoritative manner that immediately put an end to the conversation.

A hush fell over the diner as no one knew what to say or why Eden wouldn't want to talk about something as glamorous and exciting as being a model. Even I was confused. But maybe she just wanted the attention for me instead of her since it was my birthday.

"Well, thank you so much for breakfast," Eden said after a few moments, "but I have a lot more surprises for Garrett and we gotta get going."

Anabel and Darlene came over and hugged us goodbye.

"Don't be a stranger," Darlene said.

"Yeah, you better come back for Eden's birthday in a few weeks," Anabel added.

"We will," I assured them with a smile.

Next, Eden took me to the Folger Shakespeare Library on Capitol Hill. That wasn't much of a surprise. It was my favorite museum because of the sessions of contemporary poetry it featured. I wondered when the actual surprises would begin.

As we walked through the replica of the playhouse theater from Shakespeare's time, I noticed a strange redheaded girl with dark glasses staring at us.

"Do you know her?" I asked Eden after I realized the redhead was following us.

Eden looked in the girl's direction and smiled. "I'm going to the bathroom," she said as she scampered off before I could say another word.

I turned around and watched as the redheaded girl approached me slowly. It struck me how she licked her lips repeatedly.

"Hi, Garrett," she said when she stood in front of me.

"Maddie?"

## Chapter 20:
## Angel in Disguise

I couldn't believe Madison McPhee was standing right in front of me. I now understood why Eden was so determined to get me out of the house today and what she meant by surprises. I couldn't have been more surprised.

Maddie and I stared at each other for a moment. At first my mind had a hard time registering that it was really her under the wig and dark glasses, but those lips were unmistakable. I missed those lips. I ached to touch them again.

"Eden told me what happened with you and Joel. I'm so sorry, Garrett. I wish I could have been there for you. I'm glad you're okay." I couldn't respond to this. I didn't know how to. What was I supposed to say to that? She could have been there for me if she really wanted. She was just too afraid to let anyone know how she felt for me. Too ashamed to have a black boyfriend. I could have died, yet she stayed away just to keep up appearances.

"Do you like the hair?" She tried to lighten the mood as she patted her wig. "I always wanted to be a redhead. People say redheads are like fiery and brave and bold and stuff. Blondes supposedly have more fun, but I don't find that to be true. I'd rather be brave, you know?"

I nodded at her nervous rambling. I'd missed that too.

"I'm sorry I can't take it off. Someone might recognize

me." Maddie looked over her shoulder observing the other people in the library. Her gaze lingered on a huge black man standing in the corner. "That's my bodyguard, Roscoe. He's a pretty cool guy, but it took a ton of convincing for him to let me come here today."

"Why *did* you come here today?" My voice came out weak and small. I think I was still in shock from seeing her after three weeks. I cleared my throat and repeated the question in a more manly voice.

"I wanted to see you and I wanted to wish you a happy birthday. Plus, Eden has been calling me every day for like two weeks. She's a very determined little girl when she wants to be."

"I'm sorry she's bothering you. I'll tell her to stop."

"No, it's fine. She's not bothering me at all. We've started talking and getting to know each other. It's nice to have someone to talk to. I get pretty lonely on the road with my dad sometimes. I kinda wish you would call me too."

"Are you sure that wouldn't hurt your father's campaign?"

Maddie breathed in sharply like my words physically hurt her. I couldn't believe I'd said that. What was wrong with me? I'd dreamed about seeing her face for three weeks and now that I had her right in front of me I was intentionally mean to her.

"I guess I deserve that," she said. She took off her glasses and dabbed her eyes with the back of her hand. She looked at me with her incredible eyes and I felt like even more of a jerk for making those cherubic blue eyes sad.

"No, you don't deserve that. I'm sorry Maddie." I wanted to hug her, but I didn't know if that was allowed. I didn't know whether her bodyguard would leap across the room and command that I not touch her. I also didn't know whether Maddie would welcome a hug from me or not. I thought it best to just keep my distance.

"No, I *do* deserve it. I was awful to you. I must have made you feel like garbage the way I was so obviously ashamed of you. I didn't mean to make you feel that way. I'm so sorry I hurt you." She grabbed my hand and squeezed gently. "Eden tells me you've been in bed for weeks."

A surge of embarrassment flooded my emotions. Why did Eden tell her that? She made me look so weak and pitiable. Of course, that was the way I'd been acting, but the last thing I wanted was for Maddie to know that. I didn't want her to know what effect she had on me.

I shook my hand free. "You didn't hurt me. I'm completely over you. I was in bed recovering from the stab wound." I still can't believe those words came out of my mouth even though I heard them in my own stubborn, cocky voice. Pride prevented me from telling the truth. The truth being that I still wanted her with all my heart and that I would give anything to just hold her in my arms for the rest of the day.

Maddie looked away abruptly, probably to hide the tears running down her cheeks. Her bodyguard started walking our way and Maddie waved him off.

We stood in silence while Maddie tried to collect herself in order to continue our conversation. Why didn't I just reach out and put my arm around her? Why didn't I try to console her?

Finally, she put her sunglasses back on and said, "I'm sorry you're over me, because I'm not over you." Then she handed me a slip of paper. "Happy birthday."

I looked down at the paper and saw the address and phone number of someone named Peter Lawson. "What is this?" I asked. I had to repeat the question a little louder as she had already begun to walk away.

She took a couple of steps back toward me and said, "That's the police officer that was assigned to your grandfather's murder. You were on my mind so much that I started to research your parents' past like I said I would. He's retired now, but I've talked to him and he remembers the case vividly. I thought you might want to call him and finally get some answers."

I looked back down at the sheet of paper. I couldn't believe she had done this for me. I guess she really did care. But I felt it was too late to change what I had said earlier so I just said, "Thank you."

Instead of responding, she closed the gap between us and flung her arms around me, burying her face in my stomach. I'd forgotten how little she was. I instinctively hugged her back and bent down to rest my chin on the top of her head. Maddie gave me one last tight squeeze then ran away.

I stood there for a moment contemplating what had just happened. Maddie had done something so completely selfless and caring and all I had done was try to break her down with my words. How could I be so cruel to someone I loved so much? I couldn't let this be the end. I couldn't let her walk out of my life forever not knowing how I truly felt. I ran after her and caught her right before she exited the main door. I grabbed her arm and pulled her off to the side. Once we were somewhat secluded, I took off her glasses and pulled her close to me. Without saying another word, I seized her mouth in a powerful kiss.

At first I kissed her hungrily and possessively, but the kiss quickly morphed into something slow, passionate, and meaningful. It represented all that we had meant to each other and all that we still needed from each other.

"I missed you so much," she said after I'd pulled away and began to kiss her forehead, her cheeks, her eyelids, her

chin.

"I missed you too," I whispered before kissing her lips again. I held her tight against me molding her body to fit my own. I wanted her so badly. Why didn't she want me just as much?

"Will you call me after you talk to Mr. Lawson? Just call my cell phone. My father doesn't have to know. Then maybe we could meet somewhere. Maybe another museum or something. I think this disguise really works. We could probably even do dinner or something." Maddie spit out her words with ferocious velocity unable to contain her enthusiasm. Her eyes were full of hope and what I thought could possibly be love, but I wasn't sure. How could I be?

I rested my forehead on hers and sighed. A pain entered my chest. This wasn't going to work. I couldn't be in a relationship like that. I couldn't be someone's clandestine boyfriend.

"Maddie, I'm sorry. But I can't be with someone who has to put on an elaborate disguise just to be with me in public. I can't be your dirty little secret."

"But you're not. Y-you wouldn't be. I'm gonna tell him. I am."

I closed my eyes and shook my head. I thought about my parents. This was probably exactly how it was with them; my mother hiding her relationship with my father from her father. When she finally did reveal it, her father didn't accept it. Look how it turned out for them. I didn't want to turn out like my father. That's not to say I would ever consider killing Senator McPhee, but I'm sure my father thought the same thing about my grandfather. The situation just didn't feel right.

"Look, when you love me enough to make me a part of your life, come back to me. I'll be waiting for you." I kissed

her gently on the lips then walked away. She called after me, but I kept walking.

"Where's Maddie?"Eden asked when she found me sitting alone on the front steps.

"She's gone."

"But why? I have tickets for a play and I thought you guys could go together. She said she wanted to spend the day with you. Why did she leave?" Eden was on the verge of tears as she frantically fished the play tickets out of her pocket and presented them to me.

"Come here, Bug," I said as I seated her on my lap. "Thanks for trying to get us back together. It was sweet of you. But it's just not going to work."

"But why not?" Eden crossed her arms and pouted.

I sighed. I had to make her understand that Maddie and I might never be able to be together without making Maddie look bad and without making Eden feel worse. "Maddie has a lot going on in her life right now. Her father is running for president and I don't exactly fit in with the family of a presidential candidate."

Eden stared at me intently for a moment. "So, you think you're not good enough for her?" I shrugged not wanting to admit out loud what I knew to be true. "But, Garrett, you are. You're the best thing to ever happen to Maddie. She told me herself. And her father will love you once he gets to know you. Y-you just have to meet him and…and tell him how much you love his daughter. He'll accept you. I know he will."

"Even if what you say is true, Maddie isn't ready to take that step. She's not ready for me to meet her father."

"But-"

"Eden, please, just drop it. It's over."

Eden didn't feel like going to the play with me. She

claimed she was tired. Instead, we went back home ending my birthday celebration early. I didn't really mind. After my encounter with Maddie, I didn't feel like celebrating anything.

"Back so soon?" My mother asked when we entered the house. She gave us both a hug and a kiss.

"Yeah, Maddie ruined all my plans. I don't think I like her very much anymore. She's hurting my brother. She didn't even get him a real present. Just some address of some guy named Peter Lawson. What a horrible girlfriend. I'm going to take a nap." Eden marched to her room dramatically tossing her coat on the couch as she went. I was actually relieved that some of her flair had returned. It was like having a goal and working towards it had brought her out of the funk she'd been in. She reminded me of how she danced around on the metro the day she saw me writing a poem to Maddie. I felt like she was getting back to normal.

"Peter Lawson? Peter Lawson. Where do I know that name?" My mother tucked her straight blond hair behind her ears and looked pensive.

"Eden's exaggerating. Maddie and I were never boyfriend and girlfriend. Not officially anyway. So, technically, she couldn't be a horrible-"

"Detective Lawson," my mother interrupted me as a proverbial light bulb went off in her mind. "Garrett, listen to me, I absolutely forbid you from talking to him. Do you understand me? He's a crazy old man that has no idea what he's talking about," she said seriously. I should have realized that she wouldn't like me investigating my grandfather's murder. It never occurred to me that Eden would bring it up in conversation. I had just planned to see Mr. Lawson without ever telling my mother.

"What?"

"I'm serious, Garrett. Stay away from him."

My curiosity was piqued. Staying away would be the last thing I'd do.

# Chapter 21:
# Facing the Truth

I didn't want to wallow in self-pity anymore. I realized that accomplished nothing. I still wanted Maddie, but I had to find some way to get her off my mind. Peter Lawson and my mother's past were a perfect diversion.

Several different scenarios of a first meeting or conversation played in my head. Maybe my father killed my grandfather in a violent outburst after he refused to let him marry his daughter. Maybe after months of hiding their relationship, my father decided the only way he could be with my mother was to get rid of her father. Maybe my mother and father planned the murder together. Maybe my mother was actually in jail for the first five years of my life and that's why I didn't know her. No, that wasn't possible. I think I would know if my mother did jail time.

I didn't know what I expected this Peter Lawson to tell me. I guess I wanted a reason, some sort of motive or logical explanation. I wanted something that would help me accept that my father was a murderer and that my mother still cared for the man that had killed her father.

I went back to school the Monday following my birthday. I wanted things to seem normal so my mother wouldn't suspect that I was making plans to visit Detective Lawson.

He lived in North Carolina about 50 miles away from

Catolby prison, so I decided I would stop by before my next visit with my father.

I rang the doorbell of the Lawson home but wasn't sure if it sounded or not, so I knocked as well.

"I'm comin', I'm comin'," someone grunted from inside. "I'm old! You're gonna have to be patient." A few moments later, an old Caucasian man with a walker opened the door. "Who are you and what do you want?"

His abruptness startled me somewhat. "I'm Garrett…um..."

"Do you have a last name?"

I actually didn't know how to answer that. I wasn't really Garrett Anthony, but was I Garrett Whitman or Garrett Baker? I wasn't sure so I just said. "Are you Peter Lawson?"

"Yeah, what of it?"

"Um, you knew my mother, Holly Jane Whitman. I was just wondering if you remembered her."

Mr. Lawson stared at me intently. He squinted his eyes making the liver spots on his face draw together and unite. He scrunched his lips and grunted, then turned his back to me as he moved slowly back into the house pushing his walker in front of him.

I waited at the door not knowing what to do. Maybe he hadn't heard me.

"Ya feet got glue on 'em or somethin'? Get in here!" I stepped through the door into his living room. A collection of orange and brown furniture from the seventies and a musty smell assaulted my senses.

I stood in the middle of the room as Mr. Lawson maneuvered himself into an arm chair. He seemed to be having difficulty so I offered him a hand.

"I can do it myself!" he snapped. After a few more moments he had won the battle with the chair and sighed with relaxation. "That's the worst part about getting old, not being able to do seemingly normal things anymore. That, and the hemorrhoids."

I wasn't sure whether to laugh or not, so I gave an awkward smile and took a seat on the dusty orange sofa.

"How old are you, son?"

"Sixteen…um… 17."

"Well, which is it?"

"Seventeen, I just had a birthday."

"December 10th, no…ninth, right?"

"Yeah, how did you-"

"They say you never forget your first case and your last case. I'd have to agree. I was 65 and ready to retire when I was thrown into the Whitman family." He folded his hands across his chest then leaned his head back reflectively.

"I'm glad to hear that, sir, because I wanted to ask you a few questions."

"About what?"

"About my grandfather's murder."

"Your mother never told you nothin'?" I shook my head as a response.

"Yeah, I'd expect she wouldn't. Your mother was never really good at facing the truth."

Mr. Lawson began shuffling things around on the table next to his chair.

"Louise! Where are my chocolates?" he yelled in a frustrated tone.

"You've already had too many," came a female voice from the kitchen.

"I haven't had any today."

"You expect me to believe that?"

"I expect you to bring me my goddamn chocolates when I goddamn ask for 'em!" Mr. Lawson swung his fist in

161

the air as if he were punching the disembodied voice of Louise. "You see, Garrett, that's the worst part about getting old, not being able to eat your chocolates when you want to."

I let out an uncomfortable chuckle then stared down at my hands.

"Do me a favor, son, and look under that couch. There should be a box." I obeyed and dove my hand under the couch. After grabbing a few fistfuls of dust and cat hair, I felt the box and pulled it out. He gestured for me to bring it to him. Inside were miniature Hershey bars. He ate three with unabashed ecstasy before returning his attention to me.

"You look just like your daddy," he said with a mouth full of chocolate. "Except for the hair and the eyes. I guess you get that from Holly."

Not knowing what to say, I nodded like a tongue-tied idiot.

"I was there the day you were born, you know."

"You were? Why?"

"I just had to see you for myself. I gotta tell you. I ain't never been so happy to see a black baby come out of a white woman in my life."

"Excuse me?" I asked a little startled at his frankness.

"You heard me. I was happy you came out black. I probably did a little jig right there in the hospital."

"But I don't understand. Why?"

"Because it meant you were Greg's son and not Thomas'."

"Who's Thomas?"

"Boy, she really didn't tell you anything." Mr. Lawson ate another chocolate before he said, "Thomas was Holly's father."

My throat tightened and my body tensed. A wave of nausea gripped me. I hoped I misunderstood what Mr.

Lawson was saying. I hoped he wasn't telling me that he suspected my grandfather impregnated my mother.

"Are you saying that my grandfather..." My voice trailed off. I couldn't even say the repulsive idea out loud.

"Thomas Whitman was a perverted bastard that was able to hide behind his money. He had some sort of soap empire, you know. My only regret in life was that we didn't catch him in time so he could spend the rest of his life in jail. But in the end, I guess he got what he deserved anyway."

"Mr. Lawson, I'm sorry, this is a lot for me to take in. I'm afraid I don't really understand. How do you know this?"

Mr. Lawson ate another chocolate and sighed. Then he got a distant look in his eye as he started to relate his tale.

"One day, I'm sittin' in the police station and I see this pretty little blonde girl step through the door. She looks around real shy-like then flees back out. She does this two more times before finally she comes in holding hands with this massive black guy. So, I approach them, not really knowing what they could possibly want and ask what the problem is. Then, in this sweet little girl voice, she says 'my father raped me.' Well, I just about fell over. I was already old at that time and I'd hoped that I heard her wrong, but I didn't. I took them both into a room and she gave me the whole story." Mr. Lawson paused and looked at me. "I'll save you the details and just give you a general overview."

"Holly was 15 at the time," he continued, "and she told me the abuse started when she was eight. I asked her what made her come forward now and she just looked up at her boyfriend. Well, that day, a squad car went out to the Whitman estate and arrested Thomas. We brought him in for questioning and of course he denied everything and since we had no physical evidence, we had to let him go. The next day, Holly came in with her mother, Frances, and retracted her whole statement. The Whitmans proceeded to sue the

station for false arrest, defamation of character, and whole bunch of other bull hockey and they actually won.

Something in my gut told me Holly was telling the truth and that her mother made her lie, but there was nothing I could do. I tried to visit her once in a while and see if she was ready to face the truth, but she always just smiled and pretended nothing was wrong. After a while, I lost track of her. I didn't see her again until about a year later, when the call came in that there had been a shooting at the Whitman estate.

When we arrived, Greg and Holly were calmly holding each other on the floor of the dining room, while Thomas' body grew cold in the kitchen.

We took them in for questioning. Neither would talk. Then the Whitman lawyers arrived and prepared a statement on Holly's behalf. Greg didn't have a lawyer. Before I knew it, Greg was confessing to pre-meditated murder and claimed to have acted alone. He told police that Holly had nothing to do with it and that she didn't even know what he had planned. When I asked for a motive, he said that Holly was pregnant with his child and that Thomas wouldn't let them get married.

I didn't believe him for a second. I knew the murder had something to do with the abuse, but what could I do? I didn't have any evidence and Holly wasn't talking. I even suspected that the baby might be Thomas', but I hoped I was wrong. Thankfully, I was."

My hands were shaking and my mouth was dry. This was the reason, the logical explanation I'd been seeking, but it didn't make it any easier to hear. I knew there had to be some sort of terrible secret in my parents' past, but I never expected it to be as awful as incest. A gnawing pain grew in my gut. Pain from the guilt of how I had treated my mother and pain for the agony my mother must have gone through. I

164

understood her so much better now. All her life she'd been trying to escape her father's abuse by running into the arms of no-good men or by emptying bottles of alcohol and drugs. If I had known this, if I had known the truth, maybe I could have helped her in some way.

"Do you want something to drink, son?" he offered noticing my distress.

"No, I think I better...I think I'm going to...I have to go." I had to get out of there. I couldn't breathe. I bolted off the couch and headed for the door as Mr. Lawson offered words of consolation and invited me to stay for lunch.

I went outside hoping the cold December wind would keep the tears at bay, but it didn't.

## Chapter 22:
## Forbidden Love

When I arrived at Catolby Prison, my father was waiting in the visitor's area pacing. I was an hour and a half late and he seemed genuinely concerned. I ducked behind a corner and watched him momentarily. He seemed so different to me now. The amount of love it took for him to sacrifice his life for my mother touched me. I just didn't understand why he didn't tell me the true circumstances of the murder earlier. I've grown up ashamed of my father and afraid I would turn out like him. Now I admired him. I wanted to run up, give him a hug, and call him 'dad' for the first time. I wanted to thank him for saving my mother's life and giving her a chance for a normal existence. But I didn't. I think the thought of such a public display of affection with my father embarrassed me. So, instead, I casually walked over to the table and began setting up the chess board.

"Where have you been? I thought you were in an accident or something. You know you really shouldn't be driving Corbin's car without a license."

"I'm sorry I'm late. I...I had to make a stop." Afraid my face would give away what I now knew, I looked directly at the board refusing to make eye contact with him.

"You had to make a stop where? Who do you know in North Carolina?" He continued to stare at me while I tried to arrange the pieces in the same places they were a month ago.

I could feel his eyes drilling into my soul searching for the truth. He knew something wasn't right. I decided I needed to change the subject.

"Will you tell me how you and Holly met?"

The question instantly put a smile on my father's face as he probably replayed the encounter in his mind. He looked off into the distance wistfully and thought for a while.

"The summer after I turned 15," he began finally, "while all of my friends were out playing basketball, I got a job as a landscaper so I could earn some extra money. No, I didn't want to buy my first car or anything. I wanted to go to space camp in Florida. God, I was a nerd." My father chuckled for a moment. I smiled as well realizing I was more like my father than I'd thought. "Anyway, the company I worked for was doing this huge landscaping project for the Whitman family. It was scheduled to take five or six weeks to complete. My first day there, I notice this amazingly beautiful but sad girl staring down at us from her bedroom window. I asked some of the other young guys I worked with who she was and they said things like, 'Don't even think about it. She's Thomas Whitman's daughter, she's rich and unattainable, and she never talks to anyone anyway.'

"But they completely misinterpreted my intentions. I didn't want to hit on her or anything. I just wanted to make her smile. I thought a girl that beautiful should never be sad. So, after work, I took some of the flowers we had cut down and arranged them into a bouquet. I snuck up to her room and left them at her door. I did this every day for a week. Then one day she caught me. She seemed really suspicious and defensive at first as she asked me what I wanted from her. I told her that I didn't want anything, that I only wanted to see her happy. She stared at me with utter confusion as I reiterated the fact that all I wanted was to see her smile. Then a slow, timid smile lit up her face. I gave a dramatic bow and

thanked her for such an honor. She smiled even more brightly and giggled. As I turned to walk away, we both heard footsteps. She grabbed my arm and pulled me into her room, just as her father entered the hallway."

My father stopped speaking then stared at the table for a while. The pleasant wistful look on his face disappeared at just the mention of Holly's father. I wondered if he noticed something was wrong between them on that first encounter.

He cleared his throat and continued, "Before long, we were inseparable. We would meet in town and go to the movies, take long walks in the woods, have picnics by the lake. It was the best summer of my life."

It sounded like my father wanted to end the story there, but I wanted to know more. I wanted to know when he figured out that Thomas was a molester. So I asked, "Did she meet Grandma Jean? When did you meet her family?"

My father got an uncomfortable look on his face. He rubbed his forehead as if he was getting a headache. He seemed to be weighing how much information he wanted to reveal to me. He was silent so long I feared he would cut off the conversation. Then he said, "I, of course, was nervous about introducing her to my mother. We were poor and we lived in a not so good neighborhood, but Holly said she didn't care. She said she'd love me no matter what. And she did. In fact, she would come to our dingy little apartment quite often and just hang out."

"What happened when you met her parents?" I asked.

"They almost had a joint heart attack when Holly brought me home for dinner one night." He chuckled again, but I don't think it was because he found the situation humorous. I think it was a defense mechanism. He wanted to hide how much their reaction probably hurt him. "They tried to be polite and pretend like my color didn't matter, but I could tell it did. Pretty soon, Holly wouldn't be able to see

168

me because she had cotillion practice, or piano practice, or tennis lessons or she had to meet with a tutor. It was pretty obvious what was happening, but Holly wouldn't stand for it. When school started, we would email each other all day. She even bought me a cell phone so we could keep in touch. Sometimes we would skip school and meet somewhere so we could be together. We felt like Romeo and Juliet."

"So when did you find out that Thomas...." I didn't quite know how to put it. I didn't know how to come out and ask him when he realized my grandfather was a sexual predator.

"That Thomas what?" he asked with suspicion.

"That he...you know."

My father paused and stared at me. He knew I knew something. Then it hit him. "You spoke to Peter, didn't you?" He sighed as he rested his head in his hands. "I told her forbidding you to see him wouldn't work." He stood up from the table and paced the floor. After a while, he shook his head and sat back down. He must have realized it was fruitless to lie to me now.

"One night, we were in Holly's room talking. Thomas came home unexpectedly and I hid in her closet. I saw him come in and...and kiss her like a father shouldn't kiss his daughter. I froze. I didn't know what to do. I should have jumped out of that closet right then and..." My father closed his eyes and shook his head as if trying to shake the memory from his mind. "But I didn't. I didn't do anything. I felt so...powerless. I hated myself.

"Holly tried to deny what was going on, but I wouldn't let her lie to me. I'd seen the signs all along. Something inside me knew it wasn't right the way he looked at her and touched her even when I was around, but I didn't want to accept what could be happening when I wasn't there. Now I couldn't deny it any longer. After hours of convincing, she

finally told me the truth and the next day we went to the police."

"But the police didn't do anything," I volunteered.

He shook his head then said, "After the ordeal with the police and the lawsuit, Holly's parents sent her to boarding school. I was actually relieved. We were able to keep in touch and continue our romance, but she was away from her father. It gave me time to think of a way get her out of the situation."

"So when did you decide you had to take care of things yourself. When did you decide –"

My father's expression changed. He took in a deep breath and straightened his back. "That's it, we're done here," he said, standing.

"Why? What's so bad about me knowing the truth? What's so bad about me knowing that my grandfather..." Once again I couldn't finish the thought.

"You see? That's what so bad about it." My father placed his fists on the table and leaned over toward me. "It's so horrible you can't even say it out loud. Holly didn't want to make you live with that thought in your mind. She wanted to spare you from that pain."

"But now I understand her so much better. I understand you too. I think –"

"You think you understand me? You think you know me now?" My father raised his voice and a few of the other inmates and visitors looked our way. He sat down embarrassed at his outburst and drummed his fingers on the table.

"I know what kind of man you are. You're the kind of man that will sacrifice everything to protect his family and that's the kind of man I want to be," I said in a forced whisper. I didn't want to attract any more attention.

My father paused and looked at me. He jumped out of

170

his seat again, rubbed the back of his neck and paced the floor while shaking his head. He walked in silence for a while until finally he said, "I don't want you to come back here anymore."

"But why?" I asked, bolting out of my seat. I felt like he was punishing me for some reason. I finally felt close to him. I finally felt like we could have a relationship and now he was trying to cut me out of his life.

"I should never have asked you to come. It was selfish. I just wanted to get to know you. I wanted to see my son become a man. But I don't want to influence you. And I certainly don't want you admiring me and thinking that murder is an acceptable form of self-preservation."

"But I don't think that. I –"

"Garrett, I've made my decision. Now leave. I'm taking you off my visitor list and you won't be able to come back." I watched as my father turned his back on me and walked away. Then suddenly he turned again and rushed toward me. He swept me up into a bear hug and said, "I love you, son."

"I love you too, Dad."

I thought my day had gotten as emotional as possible. I never imagined it could get worse.

## Chapter 23:
## Mad Denial

When I came into the house, I found my mother clearing the dinner dishes.

"Hey, baby, where ya been?" she asked cheerily as she continued cleaning while humming a song.

I didn't respond. I just stared at her as if seeing her for the first time. She had her shimmering blond hair swept up into a high ponytail making her look 10 years younger. The tank top she'd borrowed from Eden and the fitted jeans added to the glow of youth she radiated. She looked truly happy as she bopped around the kitchen in a carefree manner. I wondered if she was in fact happy. Had she overcome the trauma of her childhood or was it all a dramatic cover? Did she love Corbin the way she loved my father? Had he provided her with everything she needed emotionally?

"Why are you staring at me like that?" she asked with a smile after a few moments.

Instead of answering her, I closed the distance between us and swept her up into my arms. I squeezed her tightly and said, "I love you, mom."

My mother giggled and said, "I love you, too, baby. But what's gotten in to you? Why am I 'mom' all of a sudden? What's wrong?" She pulled away from me and stared into my eyes. Her smile melted away as her lips began to quiver. "You talked to Detective Lawson, didn't you?" I didn't say anything, but she saw the answer in my eyes.

"Oh God. Oh God. You know don't you? I told you not to talk to him. You disobeyed me." She covered her mouth and shook her head. She looked sick. I thought she might vomit right there in front of me. "I didn't ever want you to know," she said holding back tears.

"But why not, mom?"

"Because I never wanted you to look at me like that."

"Like what?"

"Like that! Like how you're looking at me now. That pity and…and disgust in your eyes." She turned away from me and starting pulling at her hair with both hands.

"But now that I know, I feel like I can be a better son to you. I can help you."

My mother paced the kitchen shaking her head frantically. "*You* can help me? How the hell do you think you can help me? Can you erase the past? Did you read in one of your little books how to make a time machine and you can go back and fix things? You can't fix everything, Garrett. You can't fix me!" My mother turned away from me and steadied herself from the sudden onslaught of tears by holding onto the kitchen sink.

"Maybe we can get you counseling or something?"

"You don't think I've tried that?" she yelled at me. "No, no, it's a lie. It never happened," she said frantically wiping away tears and shaking her head again. "I was young and…and I made it up. He never touched me."

"Mom, please, don't do this to yourself." I couldn't think of anything else to say. What does one say when they are trying to help their mother overcome years of sexual abuse?

173

I don't think she heard me. Her eyes glazed over and she looked as if she didn't even know where she was anymore.

"Greg is bigger than me and he told me what to say. I lied to make him happy. He never touched me. He never touched me." Her voice sounded far away and rehearsed like she recited a statement.

"Don't touch me!" she yelled when I went to hug her again. She grabbed her hair and shook her head as if trying to shake out the memories.

"What's going on?" Eden asked innocently as she entered the kitchen.

"Get out, Eden! Get the hell out! Go to your room!" my mother snapped. Eden spun on her heels and ran away in tears.

"Don't talk to her like that!" I yelled. She ignored me and started opening and closing cabinets until she found some pill bottles. They were painkillers prescribed to me for my stab wound. She was going to drug herself into numbness. Now I understood her years of drug and alcohol abuse. She wanted the pain and the memories to go away. If she was high or drunk, she could escape what her father did to her. Or maybe it was simpler than that. Maybe she just wanted to die.

I lunged for her and slapped the bottles out of her hands. She fell on her hands and knees trying to retrieve the scattered pills.

"Mom, don't do this. Let me help you."

"No one can help me. I'm going to burn in hell for what I did to him. I should die. I want to die."

"What are you talking about? What you did to whom?"

"He doesn't love me anymore, does he? He couldn't possibly love me."

I had no idea what she was talking about. Whose love

174

did she question? My father's? Why wouldn't he love her anymore? He gave up his freedom for her. She had to know my father would love her forever.

I held my completely hysterical mother in my arms and let her cry. There was a missing part to this story. I could feel it. I needed my mother's version of the account, but she was in no state to tell me the truth right now.

I let her cry herself into exhaustion then I picked her up and carried her to her bedroom. As I tucked her into bed, I thought that would be the last of her strange behavior I'd see for the night. I was wrong.

I went back to Eden's room. "You all right, Bug?" I asked when I entered. She sat on the bed brushing her hair.

"Yeah. How's Mommy?"

"She's fine. She's sleeping right now."

"Did I do something wrong, Garrett? Why was she so mad at me?"

I sat next to her on the bed and put my arm around her. "It's not you. Mom's going through a lot right now. Some bad things happened to her in the past and she doesn't quite know how to deal with it."

"What kinds of bad things?" she asked looking at me with her big brown green eyes.

I sighed. I had to choose my words carefully. There were just certain things I didn't want my 11, almost 12, year old sister to know.

"Why don't you get some sleep? Mom didn't mean what she said, okay? She loves you. She loves both of us."

"Why won't you tell me what happened to her?" Eden crossed her arms and pouted.

I felt bad hiding the truth from her. I was doing to Eden the same thing my parents had done to me. I just really couldn't find the right words to use. I had trouble even saying it out loud let alone to a little girl.

"Where's Corbin?" I asked changing the subject.

"Why are you asking me? Do I always know where he is?" she snapped.

"No, I just thought since you were here you would know." I didn't understand why asking about Corbin would make her so angry all of the sudden.

"I think he might have gone back to the studio after dinner. He's got a deadline on Monday or something." Eden crawled into the sheets and shut her eyes tightly. "I'm going to sleep," she said abruptly. Her sudden lack of interest in knowing about my mother both shocked and relieved me. I didn't want to have to explain anything about sexual abuse, not after the day I'd just had. But her reaction to my question about Corbin disturbed me somewhat. What was it about him that set her on edge? I thought she liked Corbin.

I went to my room in a haze not really understanding what just happened with my mother or with Eden. Emotionally exhausted from such a trying day, I fell onto my bed and tried to sleep, but couldn't. I tossed and turned and tried to get the images of what Peter Lawson had told me out of my head. Even though he didn't go into details, my imagination took over and provided me with more than enough to put my brain into overdrive.

Staring up at the ceiling my mind drifted to thoughts of my parents and the heartache they suffered. They went through so much just to be together and I wasn't ready to make the same sacrifices for Maddie. But then again, the situation was different. My mother didn't lie to her parents about dating a black person. She had invited my father to dinner. She wasn't ashamed of him and she was willing to make him a part of her life no matter what the reaction of her parents. I couldn't say the same about Maddie. She obviously didn't love me that much.

I hopped out of bed and did over a hundred push-ups

176

trying to clear my mind and work myself to the point of exhaustion, but still didn't feel the grip of sleep approaching.

At 10:15, I decided to go for a walk. Walking didn't help either so I started to run. I ran until my chest burned so badly I couldn't think of Holly, Thomas, Peter, Greg or even Maddie.

An hour later, maybe two, I returned home and found, Eden sitting on the front steps hugging her knees.

She looked up at me with tears in her eyes. "Mom's drunk."

# Chapter 24:
# Alone

Wearing jeans and a blue North Face jacket, I approached the Ritz Carlton where the McPhee benefit was being held. Obsessed with finding out information about Maddie again, I'd read about the event all week. It was a fundraiser for the McPhee camp that offered a night of dinner, dancing, and democracy. Tickets started at $2500 each which meant that jeans and a blue North Face jacket were probably not acceptable.

I don't know what I was thinking when I went there that night. What did I expect to happen? Did I think they would look at me then usher me into the ball without a second thought? I knew that wouldn't happen. But I also knew that I needed to see Maddie. Just seeing her face would make me feel better. I told myself that if I could just sneak into the hotel and get a glimpse of her, that somehow everything would be all right. At least for a little while.

As soon as I got to the entrance, someone grabbed me, threw me against the wall and frisked me.

"This is a private function, you're gonna have to leave," he said while he gripped my shoulder with one hand. With his other hand, he brought a walkie-talkie to his lips and said, "He's clear. I'm gonna escort him off the premises." Then he started pulling me away from the hotel.

"Wait, I just want to talk to Madison McPhee. Tell her

I'm here and I know she'll see me."

"Whatever, kid. I've heard that one before. You think you're the first person to have a crush on Miss McPhee?" He continued to drag me toward the street. I thought about fighting free and running into the hotel anyway, but I didn't need to get arrested on top of my other problems. I also didn't want to cause problems for Maddie. So, I relented and let him lead me away. Then I felt another hand on my elbow.

"I got this one, Jason," a voice said from behind. "You can go back to your post."

I turned to look at my new captor and found he seemed very familiar.

"Come this way, Garrett," he said as he led me to a side door of the building. How did he know my name? Then it hit me. It was Roscoe, Maddie's bodyguard. "Wait here," he ordered once we'd entered a barren stairwell. It must've been a servants' entrance or something.

Five minutes later, Maddie came rushing down the stairs toward me.

"Garrett, what are you doing here? Are you okay?" she panted out of breath.

I wrapped my arms around her and held her tightly fighting back tears. I couldn't explain it. I was just so happy to see her and hold her in my arms again. It was the only thing in a week that felt right. Amazingly, she hugged me back even after the way I treated her the last time we spoke.

"Is it Eden?" she asked.

"It's everything."

"Do you want to go upstairs and talk?"

"Yeah, if you're not busy or anything."

Maddie let go of me and gave Roscoe a look. He nodded then went back out the door he led me through.

"He'll cover for us," she said grabbing my hand and leading me up the stairs.

179

"My dad...got me...a room...so I...ready for...ball," Maddie panted when we entered her hotel suite after climbing five flights of stairs.

"Shhh. I understand. Just sit down and breathe." I helped her to the couch then went to get her a glass of water. "We should've taken the elevator," I said when I returned and sat next to her.

Maddie shook her head. "Elevator...cameras...my dad."

"I get it." Once again it came down to her reluctance to accept me into her life. "Maybe I should go," I said, standing.

"No don't!" She grabbed my hand and entwined her fingers in mine. "We have like...an hour before...he realizes I'm gone. Let's talk."

I looked into her big blue eyes and felt the calm and assurance that I'd been searching for. Looking at her now, somehow it seemed everything was going to be alright.

"My mom started drinking again last week," I admitted sitting back down.

"I know. Eden told me."

"Corbin's been sleeping at the studio. He says he can't handle it. Eden is acting out in school and failing every class. My mother has completely gone off the deep end. If she's not screaming at us for no reason at all, she's passed out on the floor or bawling her eyes out." Maddie put her arm around me and rested her head on my shoulder. She smelled so good.

"It's like nothing's changed. I'm back to making sure Eden eats and gets to school and checking my mother's pulse in the middle of the night to make sure she isn't dead."

"I'm sorry, Garrett."

"I haven't slept in days. I don't even know why I'm here. I just feel like my life is falling apart and the last time I felt happy, the last time I felt free, I was with you. I want that again. I want you."

"Garrett, I-"

"You look beautiful, by the way." I interrupted her and changed the subject afraid of what she might say. I lifted her head and took a good look at her for the first time. I wasn't exaggerating. She was the most beautiful I'd ever seen her. She had her hair in some sort of updo with a few loose curls framing her face and she wore a red strapless ball gown. Well, Eden probably would have said it was burgundy or cherry or wine or something, but it looked red to me.

I brushed a curl out of her face then caressed her cheek with my thumb.

She grabbed my hand and gently pushed it away. "Garrett, I can't do this again. It hurts too much every time you walk out."

"Then don't let me walk out. Be with me, Maddie. I love you, okay. I love you, I need you, I want you. I can't exist without you." I felt pathetic, like I was begging her to save my life. In a way I was. At that moment, she was the only one who could save me.

Before she could respond I brought her lips to mine and kissed her deeply. At first she hesitated and tried to pull away, but I persisted. Finally, she relented and wrapped her arms around my neck. She placed her fingers in my hair and returned my kiss with intensity.

The passion between us grew quickly as we both searched to fill the void in our lives that had developed in the past month by not seeing each other. Maddie moaned as she unbuttoned my jeans making sure her lips didn't leave mine for too long. I felt around on the back of the dress for some sort of zipper or clasp, but couldn't find it.

"I'll do it," she said standing. She undid the side zipper, stepped out of the dress then joined me back on the couch. We kissed with rapacious fervor as we continued to disrobe until we were both naked and breathing heavily

burning with anticipation.

We made love quickly and passionately releasing the tension and anxiety of our lives into each other. It was animal, primal, yet completely fulfilling. It was a breathtaking physical expression of love that solidified the fact that we belonged together, we belonged to each other. Afterward, we clung to each other like we were afraid to let go.

Comfortably nestled on her warm bare stomach, I started to doze off. For the first time in a week I felt like I might be able to sleep peacefully. "I love you so much, Garrett. Please don't ever doubt that." I heard her whisper. Then she kissed the top of my head and slid out from under me. "I have to go," she said as she started to get dressed.

"Don't go. Stay with me just a little while longer." I reached my hand out for her.

"I can't Garrett. My dad's giving a speech in like 20 minutes and I need to be there. This is a huge fundraiser for him. If I'm not there, he'll know something's wrong and he'll come looking for me."

"Fine, I get it. I'll go." I angrily hopped off the couch and found my boxer shorts.

"You can stay for a while if you want. I just really need to get downstairs before I'm missed. Stay, okay? Just stay and…and I'll be back in a couple of hours."

"What good will that do, huh? You'll just make me leave as soon as your father comes within 50 feet of me. I feel stupid for even coming here tonight." Things were never going to change between us. No matter how much she said she loved me I would never be good enough for her. I would never be able to be with her the way I wanted to be.

Maddie watched quietly as I got dressed. I refused to look at her. I didn't want her to see how much I was hurting. "What do you want from me, Garrett? What the hell did you expect?" Her voice was a plea singed with frustration and anger.

"I want you to be there for me. I want you to support me. That's what I expect from someone who claims to love me."

"Why is it always about you, Garrett? What about me? You think you have the market cornered on suffering? At least you have parents who love you. My mother is dead and my father cares more about what I wear to an interview than how I feel." Maddie yelled as her shaking hands tried to pin her tousled hair back up.

"I have a stalker, Garrett. Did you know that? Did you even care to ask how my life was going? There's a creepy 30-year-old man that I've never met professing his love for me and begging to marry me. I'm not allowed to go to school, I can't go to a movie with friends, I can't even go to the bathroom without Roscoe going in first and making sure it's all clear."

I thought about what she said. Of course, she was right. I had only been concerned with my own needs. I didn't even ask about her heart condition or how her health was. I had been completely selfish.

Maddie went into the other room and quickly touched up her make-up in front of a mirror. Then she came back and slipped on her shoes as she said, "I'm sorry for everything you're going through right now, okay? I really am. But I'm going through stuff, too. And I'm sorry I can't be everything you need me to be when you need it." Maddie fought back tears as she glared at me from across the hotel suite.

"So, what do we do? Where do we go from here?"

"I don't know." Maddie took a tissue from her purse and dabbed her eyes trying to preserve her make-up. She took a deep breath and let it out slowly. Then she approached me and held me with her eyes. She kissed her fingertips then

placed them on my lips. "I gotta get downstairs."Then she grabbed her purse and left me. Alone.

# Chapter 25:
# Abandoned Again

I paced the hotel room contemplating sticking around. I wanted to apologize for not taking her feelings into consideration. I wanted to make her feel better and get her through the trying times in her life. And more than anything, I wanted to make love to her again. But I didn't want to feel like some kind of lap dog who stayed when she commanded it. My pride wouldn't let me. Even if I wanted to stay, I couldn't. Eden spent Christmas Eve with a classmate and I had to go pick her up before it got too late.

We weren't big on holiday traditions in my family so Eden spending Christmas Eve out of the house was not only okay with me and Holly, it was welcome. I thought Eden should have a chance for a happy Christmas Eve.

Eden had spent the evening with the Kobayashi family. A family with a Japanese father and a black mother. The mixture had produced four gorgeous children including 12-year-old Tracee, Eden's best friend at school.

"Eden can spend the night if she wants," Mrs. Kobayashi said when I entered their home. "She can borrow some clothes from Tracee. We really don't mind. We even have gifts for her already under the tree."

I looked over at Eden and Tracee staring at me with big hopeful eyes. They each wanted me to say yes. My heart ached. I wanted Eden to have a happy Christmas, but I also

didn't want to give the impression that something was wrong at our home. Apparently, Eden had already given that impression or Mrs. Kobayashi wouldn't be asking in the first place.

"We appreciate the offer, Mrs. Kobayashi, but we need to get home. Our mother is expecting us and…we, um, always decorate the tree together on Christmas Eve," I lied.

"We don't even have a tree!" Eden blurted.

"Eden!" I snapped and admonished her with my eyes. Eden huffed then rolled her eyes. She gave Tracee a hug, then grabbed her coat and stomped toward the door.

"Thank you for having Eden over. Maybe we'll have Tracee over soon as well."Mrs. Kobayashi gave a fake smile and a slight nod of the head. I could tell she knew that would never happen. I could tell she knew too much.

"What did you tell them?" I asked Eden through clenched teeth as we walked to the bus stop.

"I told them the truth. That my mother is an alcoholic who doesn't love me."

"That's not true, Eden and you know it. Mom loves you. She's just sick right now. But she'll get better soon."

"Whatever. Even when she's well, she doesn't love me as much as she loves you."

"What are you talking about?"

"Do you know how many times mom has raised her hand to me and you've been there to stop her? I can't even count. Well, think about it Garrett, has she ever once tried to hit you?"

I did think about it. Could Eden be right? Eden usually did get the brunt of our mother's anger.

"Eden, that doesn't mean-"

"Just forget it." Eden crossed her arms and refused to talk to me the rest of the way home.

When we got home, I knew we were in for a rough

night before I even opened the door. All the lights were off in the house and the song "A Whiter Shade of Pale" blared over the stereo. My mother hated that song. Once when Eden was four or five, Eden turned on the radio and the song happened to be playing. My mother picked up the radio and smashed it against the wall then reached out to smack Eden as if it were her fault the radio decided to play that song at that moment. Luckily, I was there to intercept the blow. My mother then went to her room and cried for hours. I hadn't heard that song since, but I knew she despised it. I wondered what possessed her to play it now.

" 'bout time you two got home," my mother slurred. She was seated on the floor resting her head on the entertainment center and nursing a bottle of scotch. "Come give your mother a hug. It's Christmas." She reached out her arms and lifted her head, but she couldn't hold it steady. She got off balance and slumped to the side spilling scotch all over the rug.

Eden shook her head in disgust then ran off to her room.

"That's right! You go to your room you little tramp. You whore!" My mother threw the bottle in Eden's direction, but it didn't go very far shattering on the coffee table two feet away.

"I hate you, you drunk bitch!" Eden yelled before slamming her door.

I went over and tried to help my mother up. "Mother, I won't stand for this. You can't talk to her that way."

"But it's true. All little girls are whores, begging men to taste the succulent fruit of their virginity." She didn't even sound like herself. My mother would never use the word 'succulent.'

"Mother, don't say that. You're not making any sense."

"Garrett, baby, do you think I'm a whore?" Her

187

demeanor changed and she suddenly seemed like a little girl in my arms begging for approval.

"Of course not, mother." She went limp. She had passed out cold. I carried her to the bedroom and tucked her in. She woke up every few moments thrashing her arms and legs wildly into the darkness then she would fall back down to the bed asleep. I stayed with her until I felt sleep had won the fight for the night.

I went to check on Eden. I wanted Eden to understand that Holly wasn't herself when she drank. We needed to come up with a plan to help our mother. By the time I got to her room, though, Eden was already fast asleep.

I lay in my bed and stared at the ceiling unable to sleep again. I closed my eyes and pictured Maddie's face hoping that the love we shared would be enough to calm my spirit and allow me to drift off. It didn't work. In fact, I felt worse because of the way things ended with us. I wanted to go for a jog, but I didn't want to leave Eden alone in the house with our mother. Her violent attitude toward Eden frightened me. I started to think maybe Eden was right. Maybe she did love me more than Eden. But how could a mother not love her own daughter? I didn't think it was possible. But, then again, with alcohol involved, anything can be possible.

Four hours later, I snuck into my mother's room to make sure she was all right. To my surprise, she was gone. I ran to the front door just in time to see her car pulling away. I stood there wondering if I would ever see her again.

## Chapter 26:
## Guardianship

One good thing about public school is that it's easy to blend into the background and not be noticed. At my old school, I was able to hide most of my problems at home. Not the case at Barton Arms. Right before Christmas break, my teachers started noticing changes in me and Eden. I started sleeping in class since I didn't get much sleep at home and Eden started mouthing off to teachers. When their requests for a parent conference went unanswered, they got our social worker involved.

"Garrett, open up. It's me, Bernice," she called as she banged on the door. It was four days before the end of break and Eden and I were getting used to fending for ourselves again. I cleaned the dishes while Eden took a shower and got ready for the day.

I don't know why I didn't answer after the first knock. I saw her car pull up and even watched as she approached the door. I just hoped she would go away if I pretended we weren't home. It wasn't that I didn't like Bernice Johnson. She had been my social worker since my grandmother died. I'd grown quite attached to her. I can remember several occasions when I begged to live with her instead of going to another foster home.

When I was five, she was only about 22 and I thought

she was the most beautiful woman I'd ever seen in my life. I wanted her to be my mother instead of Holly. Since Bernice was black, I thought my life would be easier that way. Over the years I even developed a little crush on her. When she came to see me in the hospital after my fight with Jimmy, I remember I proposed to her. She let me down easy saying that she didn't want to take me away from Eden and Holly. And that one day, when they were all right, she might take me up on that offer.

Today, she was still just as sweet and beautiful as ever, but I still didn't want to talk to her. I didn't want to explain to her that I hadn't seen my mother in days. And I certainly didn't want her putting me and Eden into foster care again. So, I continued cleaning the dishes and ignored her calls and knocks.

She was just about to leave when Eden came out of the bathroom in her robe and noticed Bernice's car.

"Bernice!" she exclaimed as she ran to the door and flung it open. She jumped into Bernice's arms and nearly knocked her over.

"Hi, sweetie," she said as she returned the hug then entered the house. "It's so good to see you."

"Here sit down," Eden said showing her to the couch. "Do you want some pancakes? Garrett showed me how to make some this morning."

"No, sweetie, I already ate, but thank you," Bernice said as she took off her coat and took a seat on the couch. "Eden, why don't you go finished getting dressed and let me talk to your brother for a while?"

Eden nodded, kissed Bernice on the cheek then bounced off to her bedroom. I dried my hands on a dish towel then went to join Bernice in the living room.

"How are you, Garrett?" she asked. She patted the seat next to her indicating that I should sit down, but I continued standing at the end of the couch.

"I'm fine. We're fine," I said crossing my arms.

Bernice nodded then pressed her lips together. After twelve years, she knew how to handle me. She knew she had to try a different approach. "You're school called me a few weeks ago. They're concerned about you and Eden." She waited for me to provide an explanation. When I didn't, she continued. "I'm sorry it took so long for me to get out here. I have about a million cases and it's Christmas time. I'm just completely swamped."

I still didn't respond.

"You're just as stubborn as ever. Richard says he hasn't been able to break through your obstinate exterior."

"I don't want to talk about Richard," I said flopping down into the recliner next to the couch.

"Why not? What did he do to you?"

"He talks to Eden about sex."

Bernice paused and pursed her lips. "Is that why you won't talk to him? Is that why you skipped your last appointment?" I didn't respond. "Look, why shouldn't he talk to Eden about sex? He's a doctor. A licensed professional. I'd rather her learn about sex from him than from her bonehead classmates."

When she put it that way, it didn't seem so bad. It kind of made sense, but I was in no mood to admit that I might possibly be wrong, so I just sat there and stared at the wall.

We sat in silence for a while as Bernice looked around the living room. I don't know whether it was the lack of a Christmas tree, the lack of cars in the driveway, or my lack of warmth towards her, but she knew something was wrong.

"How long has she been gone, Garrett?"

"I don't know what you're talking about." I hopped out of the recliner and went back to the kitchen.

She followed and said, "I'm talking about your mother

191

Holly. When did she leave?"

"She's not gone. She just went to the store to get some milk. She'll be back any minute," I said leaning over the sink hiding my face from Bernice.

"Fine." Bernice took a seat at the table. "Then you won't mind if I just wait for her. Maybe I'll have some of those pancakes, Eden was talking about."

I sighed. I knew she would stick around until the truth came out. There was no use hiding it from her. "She left Christmas morning."

"And you haven't seen or heard from her in almost two weeks?" I shook my head. "Oh Garrett, why didn't you tell someone?" Bernice stood up and embraced me.

"I don't want to end up in foster care," I said as I hugged her back and fought the urge to cry.

"Garrett, this is serious. Holly could be hurt. We need to file a missing person's report. We have to get the police involved."

"No, Bernice, please. She'll come back. She always does."

"I can't leave you two here alone. Where's your stepfather?"

I shrugged. "We don't need him. I'm 17. I can take care of Eden. Just let me handle things. I can do it. I always have."

"Garrett, I can't in good conscience-"

"Just three more days. Eden's birthday is in three days and I don't want her to spend it in foster care."

Bernice pursed her lips and drummed her fingers on the counter. She stared at me for a long time then finally said, "Here's what I'll do. I'll go talk to your stepfather and see if he'll move back in. Then I'll talk to my friend at the police station and see if there have been any signs of Holly. If that fails, I'll see if I can get you emancipated and get you permanent guardianship of Eden."

"Thank you, Bernice." I hugged her again.

"Don't thank me yet. I make no guarantees. Even if the emancipation thing works it won't be easy. You may have to drop out of school and get a job so you can support Eden."

"Whatever it takes, I'll do it."

The next Sunday was Eden's birthday. This time it was my turn to coax her out of bed. Usually, she enjoys her birthday more than Christmas which is why I didn't mind the dreadful Christmas day we'd endured. I told myself I would make it up to her on her birthday.

"I don't wanna go. I don't feel good," she said, as she curled into a ball on her bed.

"What's the matter?"

"My stomach hurts."

"Well, it'll feel better once we get to the diner."

"I don't wanna go."

"But they're expecting us, Bug. Don't you want to see Anabel and Darlene?" She didn't respond. She rolled over onto her other side and continued clutching her stomach.

I stroked her hair as I tried to think of something to say. After all that we'd been through, I wanted her to enjoy her special day. But, then again, if she was really sick, maybe she should spend it in bed. We could do something tomorrow after school.

I went to the kitchen to get working on her birthday cake when I heard the phone ring.

"Garrett?" I heard my mother's voice say. "Are you okay, baby? I miss you." I didn't respond. "I understand if you don't want to talk to me. I just wanted to let you know that I'm okay. I entered a 72-hour detox clinic and I'm feeling much better." I still didn't respond and wondered if she had really been in a clinic for 72 hours. Where had she been the rest of the time? And if she was really in a clinic,

why didn't she just tell us that before she left. I had trouble believing her. My trust in her had again been broken. "Um, I'm going to North Carolina for a couple of days to visit my mother. Will you tell Eden happy birthday, and that I love her, and that I'm sorry."

"Okay," I said numbly. I had nothing else to say.

"I have my cell phone on if you need anything."

"Okay." Then she hung up.

## Chapter 27:
## In the News

It started out as a shower. I stood with my head against the wall letting the almost too hot water pour over me nearly burning my flesh. I don't know how long I stood there, but soon, I sat down in the bathtub with my head in my hands letting the mist from the shower hide my tears.

I cried for my mother, wherever she might be. I cried for Maddie. I wanted her so badly, but couldn't have her. Finally, I cried for me and Eden. What would happen to us next? What more could we possibly live through?

Suddenly, Eden pounded on the bathroom door. The noise startled me and I nearly banged my head on the side of the bathtub.

"What?" I called. I hoped it was Bernice on the phone or something telling me that a judge was willing to let me be Eden's guardian.

"Um, something's happening on TV. I think you want to see this."

"Not now, Eden. I'll watch it later." I settled back into the tub thinking she wanted me to see some music video or some new fashion model she admired.

"No. I think you should see it, now. It might involve Maddie."

I jumped out of the bathtub, wrapped a towel around

my waist, and flew out the door. Sopping wet, I followed Eden to the living room where she pointed to the TV screen.

"It's Senator McPhee," she said.

I sat down on the couch and watched as a news channel played the same clip over and over again. It was Senator McPhee jumping into a crowd and relentlessly punching someone in the face at a campaign rally the night before.

Eden got a towel and started helping me dry my hair as I flipped to other channels. Every single one showed the same clip, some from different angles, but in each, it was definitely Senator McPhee using some man's face as a punching bag. I didn't know what it meant.

In one of the clips, I caught a split second glimpse of Roscoe pushing Maddie into a car. Then I started to put it together.

"*...this obvious lack of self-control will definitely hurt Senator McPhee's chances for his party's nomination,*" came a voice from the television.

"*Oh, I don't know about that, Susan. Maybe this country needs a president that packs a punch.*" The two correspondents shared a laugh.

All day long, people speculated about the identity of the mystery victim. Finally, that evening, the McPhee camp issued a statement. Just as I had suspected, the man Bartholomew McPhee attacked was the man that had been stalking his daughter for a month. Even though the McPhees had a restraining order against him, 33-year-old Andrew Duncan still showed up at a campaign rally in Pennsylvania. When Senator McPhee caught a glimpse of him staring at his daughter, his paternal instincts kicked in and he charged him.

The media turned it into one big joke. With flashy graphics and amusing catch phrases, they made it seem like the senator was a dangerous loose cannon that could not be trusted to lead a nation.

He had a few supporters, however. Some people stated they would do exactly the same thing if someone propositioned their 16-year-old daughter.

"What does this mean, Gary? Is he not gonna run for President now?"

"Well, he hasn't officially dropped out of the campaign yet. He still might be able to salvage his reputation."

"But his chances are pretty slim, right? Which means he probably won't win, right? Which means you and Maddie can get back together, right?"

Eden had jumped to some pretty far reaching conclusions, but I had to admit the same thoughts ran through my mind as well. It was possible, but not very likely. I turned to Eden to tell her not to get her hopes up, when for the first time that day, I took a good look at her.

"Are you feeling all right, Bug? You look a little pale."

"My stomach still hurts a little."

I reached out and felt her forehead. She didn't feel warm. In fact, her skin felt cold and clammy. "Go lie down and cover up. I'll bring you some soup, okay?"

She nodded and got up off of the couch. "If you're not better by morning I'm taking you to the emergency room," I called after her.

That night as I went to tuck her in, I noticed that her condition hadn't changed. Her skin was still cool to the touch even though she had three blankets on her bed and I had cranked up the heat. She still clutched her stomach in pain. And even though she had slept the afternoon away, she was still ready to go to bed for the night at eight o'clock. I didn't know what to do.

"I'm fine. It's just my period. I'll be better in the morning," she said when I suggested we call an ambulance.

"I don't know, Eden. Something doesn't feel right."

"Please, Gary, it's my birthday. I don't want to spend it in the hospital."

Against my better judgment, I didn't call an ambulance. Maybe it was just her period. What did I know about things like that? I let her sleep then went up to Corbin's office to use his computer. I wanted to check up on her symptoms and try to figure out if it could be something else.

I scrolled the different symptoms and diseases and found that someone her age could ail from anything, from appendicitis to lactose intolerance. I looked a little more and focused on anxiety disorder. The same stresses that caused my headaches and stomachaches when I was little could now be affecting her. Considering the month we'd had, she could definitely have developed an anxiety disorder. I reached into Corbin's desk to find a pen so I could jot down the warning signs and some specific questions to ask her and I pulled out a key instead. I set it aside and kept searching for a pen.

After making notes for an hour or so, I switched off the computer and prepared to leave Corbin's office the exact same way he'd left it. When he decided to move back in, I didn't want him to think I'd been snooping around his private materials. That is, if he ever decided to move back in. As I picked up the key to return it to the desk, I wondered what the key belonged to. I searched through a few drawers in his desk and found a lock box and the key I held in my hand opened it. My curiosity got the better of me. I had to know what was in that safe. Without a second thought, I inserted the key and opened the box. Inside was a few rolls of undeveloped film, a box of bullets, and the gun Corbin had held to Joel's head.

I took the gun out and inspected it. I'd never held a gun before. I'd seen one once when I walked home from school one night when I was 11. Some crackhead tried to sell me one. I had actually considered buying it in case Joel came back, but I didn't have the money.

Sitting there in Corbin's office holding the deceivingly heavy piece of metal in my hands, I thought about how my life would be different if I had owned a gun back then. Would I have used it in order to protect my mother and Eden when we lived in shady dangerous neighborhoods? The doorbell quickly brought me out of my dark reverie and I nearly dropped the gun on the floor. I hurriedly put the gun into the box and shoved it in the drawer. Then I returned the key to its place and rushed downstairs.

When I opened the door, I got my first shock of the evening. It was Maddie.

"I stole a car," she blurted after taking a deep breath. I stood there so completely stunned, I couldn't respond. I couldn't move. It didn't even occur to me to invite her in out of the cold. "I stole a car and I wrote my dad a letter. Well, I wrote the letter first then I stole the car and in the letter I told him about you and about me and I told him that you're black and that your father is in prison and that you've been in foster care and that you're a genius and that I love…I love you."

Maddie paused to take a breath. I still didn't know what to say so I just stepped aside and let her come into the house.

She started pacing the living room and snapping her fingers as she continued her story. "Then, while my dad was dealing with the press from the fight last night…did you see the fight? My dad pummeled my stalker guy. Anyway, while he was dealing with the press from that, I left the note in his hotel room then I took the keys to Roscoe's car and I took his car and I started driving. I stole a car." Maddie stopped to catch her breath again.

I took a step towards her to embrace her when out of the corner of my eye, I saw Eden collapse in the hallway.

"Eden!" I cried as I ran to her.

Eden lifted her head slightly and said, "I think I should

go to the hospital now. I don't feel so good." Then she leaned over and vomited on the floor.

"I'll take you. Let's go." Maddie said as she jingled the keys in her hand. I picked up my sister and carried her to the car.

## Chapter 28:
## Eden's Secrets

"Somebody help me, please!" My deep voice resonated against the cold sterile walls of the near empty emergency room. A man in blue scrubs rushed toward me, took my sister's limp body from my arms and stretched her out on a gurney. He flashed a light in her eyes and took her pulse as a woman fired questions at me.

"Are you her boyfriend?"

"Boyfriend? She's 12!"

"How long has she been unconscious?"

"She passed out in the car. About 10 minutes. She said her stomach hurts."

"Is she on drugs?"

"Drugs? She's only 12! She just turned 12 today," I tried to explain. Then I remembered it was well after midnight. "Yesterday. She just turned 12 yesterday," I explained as if it really mattered. They were too involved in examining my sister to care about what I'd said. The man and woman wheeled my sister into a room.

\*\*\*

"What did they say? What's wrong with her?" Maddie asked after she'd parked the car and found me in the

emergency room. I shrugged and placed my head in my hands. Maddie sat next to me and rubbed my back. "Don't worry, Garrett. She'll be fine."

I shook my head as I fought back tears. I didn't want to cry anymore. I was tired of crying.

"Garrett, she's strong. Think about all you two have been through, all the struggles you've overcome. She'll overcome this too." Maddie weaved her fingers in mine and lifted my hand to her lips. She tried to comfort me, but her words seemed empty and meaningless. She didn't understand.

Yes, Eden and I had been through a lot of turmoil and survived. I knew how to shield her from all our previous trials. I knew how to make sure she was well fed and prepared for school. I had succeeded in keeping Joel away from her. After what he did to me, he'd be lucky to get out of jail before she turned 18. And by then, he'd never find her. I'd make sure of that. I had kept my mother from ever laying a hand on her in one of her drunken rages. But how do I protect her from what I don't know? She was already sick. Obviously, the danger had seeped in and I wasn't there to prevent it. I didn't protect her.

After I filled out some paperwork and changed into a T-shirt Maddie found in Roscoe's car, I played word games in my head trying to distract myself from the present. I wanted to do a few push-ups, but I thought that would look strange.

I stood up and walked the halls dragging my fingers through my hair. When pacing failed to calm my nerves, I sat back down and stared at the wall.

Maddie peered at me helplessly. I felt bad for her as well, for the situation she had unknowingly found herself in. She had to be exhausted. It was at least an eight-hour drive from where the rally was in Pennsylvania. She didn't sign up to spend the night in the hospital. She had come to see me. She wanted to make things right between us. But I was in no mood or position to work on our relationship.

"Who is responsible for this girl?" The doctor demanded as he stormed into the waiting room.

"I am," I said standing up so quickly I woke Maddie who had fallen asleep on my shoulder.

"And just who are you?"

"I'm her brother."The doctor raised his left eyebrow and looked me up and down. I knew exactly what he was thinking. "Look, we have the same mother, but my father is black, her father is white. Now can you tell me what's wrong with her?"

"Hmph. I think it's time to get the police involved." The doctor turned his back to me and headed toward the nurse's station.

"Police? What the…?"I reached out and grabbed his shoulder.

I wasn't trying to hurt him; I just wanted him to explain. But the doctor reacted to the motion as a sign of aggression and yelled, "Security!"

"Wait, wait, wait," Maddie said taking my hand and stepping between me and the doctor.    "He didn't mean anything. He just really needs to know what's going on. My boyfriend is very protective of his little sister."

The doctor studied the two of us for a few seconds. He must have instantly trusted Maddie's big blue eyes. Everyone did. Including me. She had an innocence, an honesty in her sweet round face that melted away anxiety.

"Let me see some identification from both of you." I took out my wallet and handed him my student I.D. while Maddie fumbled around in her purse. She couldn't find her wallet. She dumped the contents of her bag onto the floor and searched on hands and knees.

203

"Damn it. I left my wallet," she mumbled as she turned red. Then she whipped off her necklace and stood."This has my medical information," she told the doctor holding the necklace in front of him. "There's my name and my address and my father's name if you want to call him."

"Bartholomew McPhee?" the doctor asked."Senator Bartholomew McPhee is your father?" Maddie nodded. He looked from Maddie to me then back to Maddie. He knew he needed to proceed cautiously in dealing with the daughter of a Virginia senator; especially when that senator currently occupied all the news headlines. He cleared his throat then waved off the security guard. "Do you have any contact information for your mother?" he asked me trying not to seem uneasy about Maddie's parentage.

"She's visiting her mother in North Carolina this weekend."

I reluctantly let go of Maddie's hand and I wrote my mother's cell phone number on his clipboard.

"Eden's in exam room 3," the doctor called over his shoulder as he stormed off to the nurse's station and picked up the phone.

***

Eden started crying and held her arms out to me when I entered her room.

"What's wrong with me, Gary? Am I dying? It hurts so bad."I crawled into bed next to her and held her just like I did when she was little.

"Shhh. Don't cry. You're not dying. I would never let that happen. The doctors here are going to fix you up and you're gonna be just fine." I stroked her dark blonde hair and stared into her brown-green eyes.

"You promise?"

"I promise. I would never let anything bad happen to you."Eden cried harder. She cried herself into exhaustion and fell asleep in my arms.

***

"I brought you some coffee," Maddie whispered as she entered the room. I hadn't even noticed she left.

"You don't have to whisper. She's sound asleep. Eden could sleep through a tornado."I slid out of the hospital bed then took the cup of coffee she held out to me.

"Is she okay?"

I nodded as I took a sip. It tasted wretched. I put the lid back on and placed it on the table.

Maddie hugged herself and stared down at my little sister. She was worried about her. Over the past few months, she'd grown quite attached to Eden. Unbeknownst to me, they talked nearly every day on the phone. At first, Eden just wanted to get me and Maddie back together, but after awhile I think they started to develop some sort of sisterly bond. I liked that they got along now. After that first big fight at the mall, I didn't think a cordial relationship would ever be possible between the two of them.

With Eden asleep, I finally had a moment to focus on Maddie. I stepped behind her, put my hands on her shoulders and kissed the top of her platinum blond head. Then I remembered something.

"You called me your boyfriend. You've never called me your boyfriend before."Maddie turned around and stared up at me with her blue-lake eye. She stood up straight and wrapped her arms around my neck.

Maddie ran her fingers through my long black hair and as tears welled in her eyes she said, "I love you, Garrett."

"I know you do, Maddie. And I'm sorry for ever

205

doubting it. I'm sorry for pushing you. I'm sorry for selfishly neglecting you at times. I'm sorry for anything I've ever done to make you cry. I love you, too," I said before pressing my lips to hers.

It should've been the happiest moment in my life. Madison McPhee loved me and was willing to make me a part of her life. She had told her father everything and had taken a huge risk by coming to see me tonight. But I couldn't fully enjoy the realization knowing my sister lay suffering.

I lifted her off the ground and pressed her body to mine as my mouth continued to explore hers. "What about your father? What about the election?" I asked after a breathless kiss.

"I don't care what he says. I need you, I want you, and I can't exist without you," she panted. We both smiled as she repeated the exact same words I'd told her just two weeks ago. Then someone rapped softly on the door ending our bliss-filled moment.

"May we speak to you in the hall?"The doctor asked me. When I stepped out of the room and closed the door behind me, he added, "I'm sorry I didn't introduce myself properly. I'm Dr. Shepherd and this is Rowena Smith from Child Services."

I shook both their hands and said, "I don't understand why Child Services is here?"I started to get nervous. I'd seen enough of Child Services for five lifetimes."Does this have something to do with my guardianship?"

"What guardianship?" Rowena asked.

"I'm fighting for permanent guardianship of Eden. I have to prove that I can take care of her better than my mother can. Is her illness going to hurt my chances of that?"

"We spoke to your mother," Dr. Shepherd said ignoring my question. "She faxed over a letter giving you power of attorney over Eden. She trusts you to make all the decisions concerning her welfare."That letter was worthless in my book. I'd already been doing that for the past 12 years.

"Will you tell me what's wrong with my sister, please?" Dr. Shepherd and Rowena Smith exchanged a look, a look of foreboding that instantly made my heart race.

"You might want to sit down, son," the overweight black lady said as she put her hand on my shoulder."

"I don't want to sit down. I want to know what's wrong with her."

Dr. Shepherd sighed and said, "Your sister had a miscarriage."I stared at him blankly trying to make sense of what he was saying.

"I'm sorry, you must be looking at the wrong chart. My sister is only 12. She…she just turned 12. Yesterday was her birthday."

"It's not a mistake, Garrett. We've already performed the D&C. The fetus was about six weeks old." My knees gave out and I had to grab a chair for balance. The doctor kept talking, but I really couldn't hear anything else.

"She just turned 12. We haven't even celebrated her birthday yet. She's just a child, a baby. Who did this? Who could do that to a child?"My mind was in a haze. I felt like I repeated myself over and over again.

"We need your help to figure that out," Rowena said. "Because of her age, the police have to get involved. A detective will be here in the morning. Do you know anything? Something that will help the police?"

I shook my head. I knew nothing. What kind of brother was I to let something like this happen? I should've been paying more attention to her. This was my fault and I was going to fix it.

***

I went back in to the hospital room. There was an empty bed next to Eden's that Maddie had dozed off on.

"What's wrong, Garrett?" She asked when she noted the look on my face. I couldn't respond. I think I shook my head or shrugged my shoulders as I silently crawled beside Maddie. She didn't press me with further questions. She was content to fall asleep in my arms. I watched them both sleep, the two most important people in my life. I thought about what had happened to my sister and what I was going to do about it. I knew what I needed to do.

Eden began to stir around five o'clock in the morning. I asked Maddie to leave the room for a few minutes so we could talk alone. Eden cried for me and I took her hand.

"Eden, I know something bad happened to you," I said as I tucked her hair behind her ear. "I know I let you down."

"Gary, don't cry. It's not your fault." She reached up and wiped a tear from my face.

"Tell me what happened. Tell me who hurt you."

"I can't, Gary. You'll hate me."

I crawled into bed with her again and held her in my arms. "I could never hate you. I love you more than anything in the world."

"Do you love me more than Maddie?"

"I love her differently than I love you, but yes, if I had to choose between you and Maddie, I'd choose you."

Eden sniffled and wiped her nose with the back of her hand. "Do you love me more than Mommy?"

"Yes, Bug, I do."

"That's what *he* said, too. But it was a lie. Everything was a lie."

"Who is he, Eden? Who told you this?"

"He told me he loved me more than mommy and that when people love each other that they're supposed to have sex. He said that's what you do with Maddie."

I felt like a boulder of guilt had been dropped on my chest and knocked the wind out of me. I couldn't breathe.

"It hurt so bad the first time, Gary. I thought I was being torn in two. But it got better after that and he wasn't as rough when I didn't fight back and it didn't hurt as bad. I started to accept it. I just lay there and pretended I was somewhere else until he finished. I couldn't tell you, Gary. He said it was our special secret. He said I was special."

Tears threatened to stream down my face as she spoke, but I held them back. I had to remain strong for my sister.

"One day, I went to his office expecting to have to do it again and he said we weren't going to do it anymore. He said we had to stop. I guess he didn't love me anymore."

I squeezed my eyes shut and breathed in slowly trying to gain control over my emotions. I think I already knew the culprit, but I had to hear it from her. "Eden, please tell me who did this."

"It was Corbin," she whispered before bursting into tears again. I held her tightly and let her cry on my chest. "Am I a whore, Gary?" she asked when her tears subsided.

"No, Eden. It wasn't your fault. You're not a whore."

"Mommy thinks I am."

"She was drunk. She didn't know what she was saying."

"No, Gary, she wasn't drunk the first time I told her."

I sat up and looked into her eyes. "You mean, you've already told mother? She knows?"

Eden nodded vigorously. "The night she started drinking again, when you left to go for a walk I went to her room to talk to her. When you wouldn't tell me what happened in Mommy's past I started to think maybe the same thing happened to her. I thought she could help me. I thought she would know what to do. I told her what Corbin did to me and that I thought I was pregnant and she started yelling at

me and calling me a whore. Then she threw a lamp at me but she missed. The next thing I knew, she had a bottle of alcohol in her hand and she kept yelling at me. So I went outside and waited for you."

"Why didn't you tell me this before?"

"I didn't want you to think I was a whore too. You're the only person that loves me, Gary. I didn't want you to hate me, too." She started sobbing again.

A new anger arose in me. How could my mother do this to her own daughter? She would have to pay as well. But first I needed to take care of Corbin.

## Chapter 29:
## Memory Lapse

"I remember picking up the gun. I went home and took it out of Corbin's desk. I remember loading it. I remember looking around his office. I know I found a spare set of keys to his studio taped under his desk. I don't remember driving to his studio, but I remember knowing I wanted to kill him. I know that's why I went there. I vaguely remember pointing the gun to his head. Then the next thing I know, I'm here. I don't remember firing the gun, but I know I did. Oh, God, I killed someone." I placed my head in my hands and started rocking back and forth in the hard wooden chair.

"So, you're still claiming you don't remember the shooting? You're still gonna play dumb?" The young black detective leaned back and folded his arms as he eyed me skeptically. I didn't know his name. I wasn't even sure if he was a detective. I just assumed so because he seemed like a cop even though he wasn't wearing a uniform.

Still? Why did he say 'still'? I felt like I had just woken from a coma. My head ached and my eyes burned. My mind floated in a dense fog of uncertainty. I didn't know where I was or how I got there. I assumed I was under arrest for Corbin's murder so I just tried to cooperate as much as possible. That proved harder than I thought.

The detective kept staring at me waiting for me to elaborate or something. I didn't know what else to say. I tried to jump start my memory by thinking of Eden, Maddie, and the hospital, but that just reminded me of what Corbin had done to my sister. Then the desire to kill him would arise again. I wish I could remember shooting him. I would love to see his face and the fear that no doubt consumed him, to see the bullet pierce his brain and end his life.

"If you're trying to protect your mother-"

"My mother?" I interrupted him and looked up sharply. "What does my mother have to do with this?" The last thing I remember learning was that she'd known about Corbin abusing Eden and how she did nothing. She let her only daughter be raped and just traipsed off to North Carolina. The mention of her rekindled my urge to deal with her as well. Perhaps just as cruelly as I had dealt with Corbin. Or, at least as cruelly as I thought I dealt with Corbin. What the hell happened to me? Why couldn't I remember?

The officer's eyes grew wider, maybe out of shock, maybe out of confusion. I couldn't tell. He bit his lip then tilted his head as he pinched his chin. The detective stood, adjusted his suit and began to pace the interrogation room.

"So, you don't remember that your mother was at the studio with you? The both of you were found with blood splatter on your clothing."

"My mother?" I shook my head. I had no idea what he was talking about. "Are you sure my mother was there? She couldn't have been there. She's in North Carolina."

He stopped pacing. "Garrett, what day is it?" He placed his fists on the table and leaned toward me. He studied my face while waiting for an answer.

I paused for a moment thinking this had to be some sort of trick question. Why would he be asking me something so simple? "Monday," I said finally, "January eighth."

His eyes widened again. He straightened his posture then left the room. He failed to close the door completely and I overheard voices from the hallway.

"*I don't think he's faking,*" I heard him say.

"*I told you that two days ago. It's like his ego has split and the person in that studio was not him,*" a female voice said. "*I think we should get psych down here to evaluate him again.*"

"*But if he is diagnosed as crazy, we might not have a case against him or the mother. His confession is garbage.*"

"*Maybe there shouldn't be a case against him at all.*" The woman paused. "*Let me talk to him again,*" she said. A second later she entered the room. "Hi, Garrett, I'm Marcy. Do you remember me?" Marcy had long brown hair and a warm smile. She took the seat across from me then folded her hands on the table. I looked at her carefully and tried to think of where I might have seen her before, but nothing came to me. I shook my head. She nodded and continued, "I'm the officer that brought you down to the station and booked you on Monday."

"Monday? Isn't today Monday?" I asked. "Wait a minute. What's going on? What day is it?"

"It's Wednesday, Garrett. You were arrested Monday morning for the murder of your stepfather."

"Why don't I remember? What does my mother have to do with this?"

Marcy sighed. "Do you know Richard Fielding?" I nodded. "Well, he seems to think that you've had what's called a psychotic break. In an effort to deal with some traumatic event, your mind has basically shut down and blocked it out."

I thought about this for a moment. Was it possible that Corbin's murder was so disturbing that my psyche couldn't handle it? What had I done?

213

"Where are Eden and my mother?"

"Eden is currently in child protective services. Your mother is in a holding cell a few doors down."

"I want to see her."

"Your mother? I think I can arrange that if-"

"No, Eden. I want to talk to my sister."

"I'm not sure if I can do that. She's pretty…traumatized. She hasn't spoken a word since she found out Corbin was killed."

I put my head in my hands. I thought I was helping her. I thought by killing Corbin I could make her pain go away. Now, I bet she blamed herself for his death.

Marcy stood and walked around to my side of the table. "Garrett, I want to help you," she said as she put a hand on my shoulder. "But you have to help me as well, okay? A lot of the officers here think you're faking it. That's the only reason we haven't transferred you to a mental institution. But, really, I don't want to send you to an institution. I don't think you belong in one. You've been through enough. I just need you to try really hard to remember what happened, okay? Just tell me what you know. Try to remember."

"Garrett, you don't have to tell her anything," a booming voice said upon entering the room.

"Senator McPhee?" Marcy asked, confused by his presence.

"I was a lawyer before I was a senator and I'll be representing Mr. Whitman. Now, if you don't mind, I'll have to ask you to give me and my client some privacy."

Marcy looked back and forth between me and the senator trying to make sense of the situation. I'm sure she tried to figure out why a presidential candidate would want to defend me in a murder trial. I guess she couldn't come to any logical conclusion as she shook her head and left the room.

"Sorry I took so long to get here. I wasn't sure if I

214

would do this or not." Senator McPhee sat at the table and opened his briefcase while I stared at him in utter confusion.

"I don't understand. Why are you…how did you…?"

"Madison has told me everything. I know about you and Eden. I know what Corbin did. And after some soul searching, I decided to help you."

"But, I can't pay you."

The senator's blue eyes warmed as he looked at me and said, "I'm not doing this for money." He took a pen from behind his ear and tapped it on the desk while thinking of what to say. Then he smoothed the sides of his salt and pepper hair and sighed. "I'm not even doing this for you. I'm doing it for me. I am afraid of what I would have done if put into the same situation."

We stared at each other in knowing silence. I could see in his eyes that he knew I killed Corbin, which is why what he said next surprised me.

"The way I see it, we have two major goals to accomplish. First, we have to get you acquitted of a murder charge, and second, we have to get you custody of Eden. The second task may prove more difficult than the first since you obviously didn't kill Corbin."

"What? Of course, I killed him. The last thing I remember is going to get the gun so I could do just that."

Senator McPhee shook his head. "No, Garrett, you didn't kill Corbin. Your mother did."

# Chapter 30:
# Our Eden

"Holly? My mother? She's in North Carolina. She couldn't have done it." I said, bolting out of the chair.

"She *was* in North Carolina," Senator McPhee explained. "But when she got the call from the emergency room, she started driving back. She went straight to Corbin's studio. According to her, she got there in time to see you fire a warning shot in the air. Then you apparently vomited and dropped the gun. She grabbed the gun and shot Corbin six times."

I shook my head furiously. "No, that's not true. It can't be true."

"Can you tell me with absolute certainty that it didn't happen that way?"

"I...I..." I sat back down. Since I had no memory of that day, I couldn't say for sure what really happened, but I knew with everything in me that I had been the one to kill him. I had to be. Something inside me needed to be the one that protected Eden.

"That's what I thought." The senator took out a sheet from a folder. "The evidence supports your mother's statement. According to the police report, a bullet was found in the ceiling and your vomit was found next to the body."

My mouth suddenly turned dry. I couldn't speak. Was

this possible?

"You really don't remember?" he asked. I shook my head. "I really wish you could remember. It will help with the custody battle. No judge is going to want to give a child to someone who has just suffered a psychotic break."

The senator stared at me with raised eyebrows. He wanted me to make some sort of conclusion, to come to a realization of my own. Then it hit me.

"You want me to lie? You want me to corroborate my mother's story so it doesn't look like I'm crazy?"

He nodded. "That might be the only way you can get Eden."

I put my head in my hands and took deep slow breaths. "I can't send my mother to jail on a lie. I don't really know what happened."

"Look, Garrett, your mother already confessed. The police have their murderer. The most they can pin on you right now is conspiracy or accessory. I'm sure they'll be willing to drop the charges if you cooperate."

"I don't know if I can do that."

The senator loosened his tie then whipped off his expensive looking suit jacket. "Look, Garrett, Eden's father is in jail. Holly is going to jail as well for possibly a very long time. Your grandmother, Francis Whitman, doesn't want her. I already checked. All Eden has is you. What is she going to do if you go to jail as well? Where will she go?"

Years in politics had certainly honed Senator McPhee's skills of persuasion. I actually considered lying to the police and claiming I remembered the shooting.

I thought about my sister's plight. She definitely needed me and I needed to be there for her. But could I really send my mother to jail for something I quite possibly did myself?

I didn't know what to do. I stood up from the table and

paced the room.

Finally, I said, "I need to talk to my mother."

My mother crossed the cell and embraced me as soon as I entered. I didn't know whether to hug her back. I wasn't sure where we stood. She had abandoned me and my sister leaving us to fend for ourselves. She had ignored the fact that her daughter had been sexually abused instead of protecting her. My mother had failed both of us so many times I couldn't keep track. Was she now trying to redeem herself by claiming she killed Corbin when she didn't?

She noticed my cold reception and slowly let me go. "I'll understand if you hate me for the rest of your life. I've been a pretty awful mother, especially to Eden." My mother wiped tears away with both her hands then took a seat on the bench that jutted out of the wall. I continued standing as I glared at her. She looked deathly pale except for the puffy red circles that had formed around her eyes. Her normally shimmering golden blond hair hung dull and lifeless down her back. She'd aged years since the last time I'd seen her either from two weeks of drinking and alcohol abuse or from the current stress of a murder charge.

"I think a part of me always loved you more, Garrett. I never really realized that until recently." She tucked her hair behind her ears and looked up at me. Why was she telling me this? It wasn't helping the situation. I loved Eden more than anything in the world. For my mother to tell me she didn't feel the same way did not raise my opinion of her.

Is that why you let Corbin rape her? You didn't love her enough to protect her?"

"Garrett, that's not-"

"She told you weeks ago and you did nothing!"

"I did do something! I...I killed him. I protected her. I finally acted like her mother." She stood and tugged on my shirt while pleading like a child searching for approval.

I grabbed her wrists and stared at her trying to read her expression. Did she really believe she killed Corbin? I knew with everything inside me that I had pulled the trigger. But how could I be sure? Maybe I just *wanted* to be the one. Maybe I really didn't do it.

My mother sensed my uncertainty. "You still don't remember, do you?" I didn't respond. I continued holding her wrists and staring into her eyes, the eyes that were exactly like mine, and tried to extract the truth from them. "Garrett, baby, you didn't do it." She wrapped her arms around me and hugged me again. "You're innocent, baby, you can go on with your life. You can take Eden and…and be free, be happy. Forget about me."

I gave in and hugged her back. She broke down and sobbed in my arms. "I can't forget about you. You're my mother." I knew I should probably hate her for all that she had put me and Eden through, but I couldn't. I loved her and something inside me would always love her.

"Listen very carefully," my mother whispered into my ear as we embraced. Her tone had suddenly changed. She was no longer sad, tearful, and almost irrational. She sounded firm, determined, and completely lucid. For a moment I thought she had faked the entire episode including her new declaration of love for me. I started to pull away thinking my mother had transformed into some monster with a double personality when she pulled me closer and whispered, "You arrived at the apartment above Corbin's studio at 7:15 in the morning. You woke him up with a gun shot into the ceiling. When he jumped out of bed, you pistol whipped him to his left temple. He fell to the floor unable to get up. The sight of the blood on his face made you nauseous so you puked and dropped the gun. He reached for it and you kicked it away."

My mother paused as a uniformed police officer walked past the cell. He eyed us suspiciously until my

219

mother let me go and we separated.

"Mom, why-"

"Shh!" She interrupted me. She waited until she couldn't hear any more footsteps, then hugged me again and continued to whisper in my ear. "That's when I came in. I grabbed the gun then shot Corbin in the crotch, then in the head, then four times in the face."

Though my mother said these words with conviction, I still had a hard time believing her. I hated to think that I was so weak that I would vomit at the sight of blood. And if I had witnessed something as gruesome as Corbin getting shot in the face four times, surely I would remember it. But then again, maybe that was exactly why I couldn't. Maybe it was too gruesome to endure.

"I was wearing my pink cashmere sweater and a pair of winter white pants."

She continued to give me details of the shooting until the police officer came back and said, "All right, that's enough. Garrett, come with me." He seemed irritated that we were still hugging, like instead he wanted us to fight and reveal a new piece of information for the case. That was probably why they let me be alone with her in the first place. They wanted to see how we interacted and if there was anything more to the story my mother had fed them.

My mother clung to me as the officer had to physically separate us. "Take care of our Eden," she called as her hand slid out of mine. "She needs you more than she's ever needed me."

Those last few words hovered in my mind. It struck me the way she said "our Eden" she'd never referred to her that way before. But really, she was ours. Though my mother gave birth to her, I had been the one to raise her. I saw her take her first steps, I taught her to read, I tucked her into bed nearly every night of her life. She learned to say my name

before she said 'mama' and whenever she had to fill out a form or something for school, she always listed me as her guardian instead of Holly.

Eden looked to me for protection, guidance, love, and security. In the past few months, I had failed her, but I would never let that happen again. I would be there for her for the rest of her life even if it meant sending my mother to prison.

## Chapter 31:
## Finally Family

It wasn't hard to prove what Corbin had done to Eden. Even though she still refused to talk, the investigators didn't need to hear what happened. The DNA from the dead fetus proved with 99.7% accuracy that Corbin was the father. Given this evidence, the district attorney showed my mother leniency and allowed her to plead guilty to voluntary manslaughter instead of charging her with first degree murder. I'd hoped that the judge would also be lenient and give her a reduced sentence, but that didn't happen.

The judge sentenced her to eight years in prison with eligibility for parole in five. He felt that my mother couldn't claim the knowledge of Eden's abuse fueled her actions since she knew weeks beforehand.

At the sentencing, my mother resigned to her fate and showed no emotion. The way she nodded in quiet acceptance made it seem like she wanted to go to prison. I think she felt she needed to pay for all the years she was an inadequate mother.

Eden didn't attend the hearing. In fact, she rarely left her room at the foster home where she now resided. I had succeeded in earning my emancipation and therefore did not need to live in a foster home again. But I wasn't able to get custody of Eden just yet. I had to prove to the judge that I could take care of myself and provide a stable home for my little sister.

Senator McPhee let me stay in his condo in DC while I got a job and saved up enough to rent my own apartment. During the day I worked as a bicycle messenger for an accounting firm and in the evenings I worked as a busboy in an Italian restaurant. On the weekends I spent all my time with Eden trying to get her to open up to me.

Working 16-hour days during the week and camping out in Eden's room on the weekends left me very little time to spend with Maddie. Not that it mattered since she still accompanied her father on interviews across the country as he tried to salvage his political career. He'd given up his run for the presidency, but he still sought support for his new foundation that attempted to protect young girls from sexual predators. Maddie and I talked on the phone as much as possible and took full advantage of the few times she came into town. Our relationship had developed into so much more than a high school crush and even went beyond first love. We knew we would always be a part of each other's lives no matter what the future held.

Senator McPhee understood our connection and he never tried to hinder our relationship. Maddie felt silly for ever hiding it from him. He accepted me into their family without a second thought. He did, however, advise that we take it slow and not pressure each other into a lifetime commitment while we were both still so young.

After four months of saving every penny I earned, I finally had enough money to rent and furnish a small apartment in Manassas, Virginia. I also got my license, bought a car, and took the liberty of registering Eden in a nearby school. Now I just needed the judge to award me temporary custody so I could prove I could take care of her.

Then maybe I could have permanent guardianship.

"The next time I see you, we'll be in the judge's chambers," I told Eden one Sunday afternoon. I had just finished reading to her some poetry from Maya Angelou hoping to spark some sort of reaction out of her, but to no avail. Eden had continued her catatonic stare out the window the entire morning. "Judge Garner is going to decide whether or not you can come live with me."

Eden looked at me for the first time that day. She didn't need to speak for I knew what she wanted to say. She wanted to know if there was really a chance that she could get out of this place and go home with me.

"I've been working so hard, Eden, to prove that I can take care of you. I think the judge will see that. I think I have a pretty good chance."

Eden reached for a pen and paper off the bedside table and wrote: *You mean you still want me?* The question tore at my soul and made even my bones ache. How could she ever doubt that I would want her in my life? What had that monster done to her self-image?

I embraced her and said, "You're my baby sister. You mean everything to me. Of course, I want you."

That afternoon, Bernice came over to my apartment in order to evaluate it and report back to the judge, "Everything looks great, Garrett. You've really done a wonderful job proving your competence. I'm proud of you."

"Thanks, Bernice." I smiled inside trying not to reveal just how elated I was to hear her say that. "Maddie helped me decorate this room. Purple is Eden's favorite color," I said as we walked into what would be Eden's bedroom.

Bernice smiled at the purple walls then sat on the bed and picked up a large pink butterfly pillow. "Eden would definitely love this room," she said staring at the pillow.

I didn't like the uncertain way she said 'would.'

"Why did you say it like that? Is there something I should know?"

Bernice sighed. "It's just that. I don't want you to get your hopes up. Don't get me wrong, you've done a great job over the past few months proving you can pay bills and take care of yourself, but let's face the facts here. You're 17, you have a questionable mental health history, you haven't finished high school, and you're working so many hours to make ends meet, when would you ever be home for your sister?"

I leaned against the dresser and stared at the bottles of body spritz and glitter lip gloss that Maddie insisted Eden needed. What would I do if I couldn't have my sister with me? I couldn't let her stay in a foster home for the next six years until she turned 18. I would kidnap her and run away before I let that happen. But then what kind of life would that be for her?

"I'll do the best I can, okay?" Bernice squeezed my shoulder before exiting the room and leaving me with my thoughts.

Six o'clock the next morning, I opened my front door on my way to work and found Maddie on the ground searching through the contents of her purse.

"Garrett!" she whined as if I'd just spoiled her surprise. She closed her purse and stood up. "I think I lost the key you gave me."

"What are you doing here? I thought you were in Texas this week."

"I was, but my dad let me fly out here so I could be with you on your big day." She jumped into my arms. I swung her around while planting kisses on her neck. "Wait a minute, wait a minute," she said as she unfolded herself from my arms. She looked at my bike messenger outfit and said, "Where are you going?"

"I have to go to work."

"But it's the day of the hearing."

"Yeah, but that's not until three o'clock. I figured I can put in a few hours of work then change and get to the judge's chambers in plenty of time."

Maddie stared at me in disbelief. "Garrett, this is possibly one of the most important days of our lives. You can't-"

"Our lives?" I repeated with a slight grin.

"Yeah, our lives, I mean, I plan on being a part of your life for like a really long time. That is, if you want me to be, of course. And Eden is a part of your life so I figure she's a part of my life too. I mean if you get custody of her and we get married one day or something...I mean, I'm not saying we're gonna get married or anything. I mean, not any time soon at least. Not that I don't want to marry you or anything. I'm just saying...well, I don't really know what I'm saying but-"

I silenced her nervous rambling with a long kiss.

Several moments later, we pulled away both flustered and flushed. Maddie smiled and licked her lips. "Well, in any case," she continued once she relaxed somewhat, "you can't just show up all frazzled and sweaty from work. You need to make this day special for you and Eden. I thought we could pick her up and spend the day together. I have it all planned out."

Maddie's plans actually had very little to do with me. After we picked up Eden and had breakfast, Maddie whisked her off to a beauty salon for some pampering. I didn't realize how much Eden had let herself go until I saw how beautiful she looked after a haircut and new outfit.

Maddie's beauty makeover really did wonders for Eden's mood. I saw a glimmer in her eyes that I hadn't seen in months. She actually smiled when I complimented her.

226

Maddie helped restore some of the self-esteem Corbin had stripped away.

At three o'clock, Eden and I sat in Judge Garner's chambers along with Bernice and Henry Lattimer, the lawyer Maddie's father recommended.

After Bernice recounted all the steps I had taken in order to win custody of Eden, the judge sat silent as he read over some files.

"For a 17-year-old boy suddenly thrust into adulthood, you've done a remarkable job." He paused and breathed heavily. "I'm just not sure that placing a 12-year-old in your care is the best thing for either of you. You still have a lot of maturing to do. And Eden really needs the help of trained professionals. She hasn't spoken in nearly eight months. I don't want to make matters worse for both of you. I want to make sure you both have a chance to lead normal productive lives considering all you've been through."

"What about what *I* want?"

Every head turned slowly in search of the tiny feminine voice that spoke those words. We were all shocked to realize they came from Eden.

"What do *you* want, young lady?" the judge asked in a calm grandfatherly tone.

"I want to live with my brother. Please let me live with my brother. He's all I have." Eden put her face in her hands and sobbed as I wrapped my arms around her.

I saw Bernice wipe tears away and even noticed that the judge and Henry seemed affected. They each cleared their throats and adjusted their seating positions.

After Eden's emotional outburst, the judge reconsidered. He decided that living with me might be the best thing for her since we were obviously so attached to one another.

Eden didn't even want to go back to the foster home to

collect her few belongings. She wanted to go straight the apartment, to her new home. Maddie greeted us with balloons, festive decorations, and a table full of Eden's favorite foods. Then we sat together and ate dinner as a family.

## Epilogue:
## A Mother's Love

*Five years later...*

The same dream plagued me night after night. I saw blood, I heard screams, I even smelled a sickening odor that often sent me running to the bathroom in the middle of the night to vomit. The closer we got to my mother's parole hearing the more intense the dreams became.

"You okay, Babe?" Maddie knelt next to me in front of the toilet and rubbed my back.

I nodded. "I'm fine. Go back to sleep. You have class in the morning."

"I'll skip it if you need me." She kissed the side of my head and brushed my hair out of my face.

I shook my head and held back the urge to vomit as another image of Corbin's bloodied corpse flashed in my mind.

"I'm really worried about you, Garrett. Maybe we should take a vacation or something until after Holly's parole hearing."

"I can't take Eden out of school for a week. It's her senior year. And I'm not going to leave her here alone when my mother might be getting out of prison in a few days."

"Okay, okay," she kissed my cheek and continued to stroke my hair. "Just tell me what you want me to do and I'll do it."

"You've already done so much for me and for Eden. I don't know if I could have gotten through the last five years without you in my life." Maddie smiled as her eyes welled with tears. I had to turn away from those eyes. They had too much control over me. I might not be able to do what I needed to do when the time came. "Just promise that if anything happens to me, you'll always be there for Eden."

"Garrett, what are you talking about?" She stopped smiling. A tear rolled down her cheek. I didn't really know what I was talking about. I just felt with everything in me that there was a missing piece to Corbin's murder. And that the missing piece was me.

The next day, I got a package in the mail. It was a video tape and a letter from Dashanka. After a momentary mental lapse, I remembered Dashanka was the other photographer that worked at Corbin's studio. I wondered what she could possibly want after five years.

*Dear Garrett,*

*I hope you and Eden are doing well. I know this letter may come as a surprise after so long. I've written this letter probably a hundred times and then ripped it up. I probably won't send this one either. Let me get to the point. A few days after the police cleared the crime scene, I was doing some remodeling of the studio in preparation to sell it. I could never work there again. Anyway, I found a hidden surveillance system that Corbin had installed. On the hours of footage, I learned what a despicable person Corbin really was. I know you know this already and this is not why I'm writing you. There was something else on the tape that I thought you might want to see. It is the only copy. Do with it what you will.*

*Dashanka*

The instant I watched the video, it all came flooding back…

After I left the hospital, I went home and up to Corbin's office. I took out the gun and loaded it. I'd never loaded a gun before so I imitated what I'd seen on TV. Next I looked around his office for a set of spare keys to his studio downtown. I knew there had to be a set somewhere. After trashing the office for a few minutes I found them taped underneath the desk.

The sun had already risen and I hesitated at the door of Corbin's studio. I knew someone would see me enter. I would be easily identified and arrested for the murder I was about to commit, but I didn't care. I had to do this. If I didn't, I'd never sleep again, I'd never be able to look at myself knowing that I let Eden's rapist live. He didn't deserve to take another breath.

I turned the key and opened the door. My photographic memory proved useful as I disabled the alarm by punching in the code I'd seen Corbin use. I didn't want him to know I was coming. This had to be a surprise attack.

I climbed the stairs to the little apartment he had above the studio. My stomach churned at the idea that this could have been one of the places where he raped my 11-year-old sister.

I stood over his bed and pointed the gun directly at his face. He must have felt my presence because he opened his eyes and fell off the bed in terror.

"Jesus, Garrett, what are you doing?" He scrambled to his feet, but I knocked him back down to the ground with the butt of the gun. "Garrett, let me explain," he pleaded. He touched his scalp and his eyes widened when he found blood. He knew why I was there. He knew what he had done.

"Don't talk to me. You don't get to speak to me!" I yelled as I lifted my arm ready to strike him again.

231

Corbin covered his head with his arms like a coward. "But I…I saved your life. You at least owe me…Just let me say something." He rose to his knees and begged me.

I paused as I thought about the day Joel stabbed me. Surely, he would've killed me if Corbin hadn't been there. But that didn't give Corbin the right to try to explain away his actions.

Corbin took my hesitation as an opportunity to speak.

"I love her, Garrett, I do. She's like a perfect little angel to me. I realize I was wrong to take her the way I did and I'm sorry. It only happened once. Then I couldn't do it anymore. I…I made myself stop. That's the real reason I moved out. Please, don't kill me, Garrett. I need help." Corbin put his face in his hands and cried. I almost felt sorry for the pitiful excuse for a man in his underwear on his knees begging for his life. I *almost* felt sorry, until I realized he was lying.

"Shut up. Stop crying!" I fired a bullet into the ceiling. Corbin covered his mouth and tried to hold in his weeping. "You're lying. Eden said it happened more than once." I pointed the gun at his head. Corbin trembled. My chest heaved with heavy breaths. The gun began to slip in my suddenly sweaty hand. I thought I would be able to just barge into his room and blow his head off without faltering, but taking a human life proved harder than I imagined.

"Please, just tell me what you want me to do. I'll do it. Just don't kill me."

Oh, I would definitely kill him, but not just yet. I tightened my grip on the gun and said, "I want you to suffer. I want you to feel the pain you caused my Eden."With that, I pointed the gun to his crotch and fired. His eyes bulged as he let out the most blood boiling, heart twisting scream.

A wave of nausea overwhelmed me as I saw the blood pooling on the floor. Corbin cried and yelled hysterically as

he writhed in pain.

I felt my knees weaken. Murder wasn't as easy as I thought.

I cocked the gun again and prepared to take another shot but couldn't hold back the nausea any longer. I leaned over and vomited on the floor. I had to get this over with before I lost my resolve.

I pointed the gun at his head again and fired.

In the movies and on TV, they don't show how gruesome death really is. I'm ashamed to admit it, but when I saw the bits of brain spill out of his head, I almost fainted.

I dropped the gun in front of Corbin's body and stumbled out of the door. I held onto the railing for support as I slowly descended the stairs. Then I stopped dead in my tracks as I saw my mother coming towards me.

"What have you done, Garrett? What did you do?" she yelled as she ran past me and into Corbin's studio apartment. She gasped at the bloody scene.

"What did *I* do? What did *you* do? Eden told you that he raped her and you did nothing!"

"I know," she said calmly. Too calmly. Her demeanor scared me. I heard sirens in the distance. My mother picked up the gun. Was she going to shoot me? "I know," she said again before emptying the clip into Corbin's already lifeless body.

"Why did you do that?"

"Get out. Get out now before the police-"

It was too late. The police barged in and handcuffed us both.

I killed Corbin. Deep inside I knew I had and after five years, I finally remembered. I remembered every disgusting detail. Now I wished I didn't. Now I realized my mother had just spent five years in prison for something I did. But that was about to change. I had to tell the police the truth, but first

I had to talk to my mother.

***

One look at my face and my mother knew my memory of that night had returned.

"It's too late, Garrett. Please don't go to the police. They won't believe you anyway," she said as she took a seat across from me in the visitor's lounge. She began nervously fidgeting with her hands and glancing around suspiciously. She seemed strung out. I wondered if she'd gotten into drugs again during her incarceration. That would definitely hurt her chances for parole.

"Why did you do it mother? Why did you lie? Why did you make me lie?" I wanted to reach out, grab her and shake the truth out of her, but touching wasn't allowed at the Westbrook Corrections Facility for Women. A guard tapped her gun to remind me of that when I took a step closer to my mother. I stepped back and sat in the seat provided.

"There's something you should know," she said as she started tapping her foot on the floor. She sighed and bit her bottom lip. "The first time the abuse from my father escalated from just touching to sex, I was about 10 years old. He was in his study having a drink and playing that God awful song that I hate. You know, the Whiter Shade of Pale one. Then he came to my room and undressed me and got on top of me." My mother paused and tried to swallow away the tears. "I called for my mother. I screamed for her and begged her to help me. She came to my room. I could see her through the partially open door. I thought she would help me and get him off of me, but instead she closed the door. Then she went and turned the music up to drown out my screams.

"A few years later when I asked her why, she said that it was my fault. That I was too beautiful. That I teased my father with 'the succulent fruit of my virginity.' She called me a whore.

"I hated myself. I felt like nothing. I was convinced she was right until I met your father. Then for the first time in my life, I felt like someone. He gave me confidence in myself and the hope that I could one day be happy.

"When I got pregnant with you I was so excited. Greg and I made plans to run away and get married. I could practically see myself staying home taking care of our beautiful child everyday while Greg went off to college. He was so brilliant, you know. Just like you. I wanted him to go to college so badly. I didn't want to …I didn't plan on ruining his future."

My mother stood and checked her pockets with shaking hands. She was looking for a cigarette. "Linda, you got a smoke?" she asked the inmate at the next table. Linda simply shook her head and continued talking to her visitor.

My mother sat down again and began chewing her nails. She rocked back and forth silently while staring at a point on the table. I wasn't sure she would continue until she said, "Then one night I came home and my father was drunk and playing that song. I knew he was going to attack me. I didn't want him inside me tainting the perfect love that you represented.

"I went to his study, got his gun and I…I shot him. Then I called Greg."

"*You* killed your father?"

She nodded. "Greg didn't want you to be born in jail, so he took the blame."

I couldn't speak. I could barely breathe. My father was serving a life sentence for something he didn't do.

"So, you see, Garrett, no matter what you *think* you did, I'm the one that deserves to be here, not you. You…you're having false memories. I've read about things

like this. You want it to be true so badly that you're imagining it."

"No, mother, I have proof. Corbin had a hidden camera in his room."

Holly's eyes bulged. "Who else knows about it? You can't tell anyone, Garrett, you can't! I swear to God, I'll kill myself. If you tell anyone Garrett, I'll kill myself. Do you want to be responsible for that?" My mother stood up and leaned toward me. The guard came forward to restrain her.

"Don't do this to me, mother. Don't make me choose between you and what's right."

My mother calmed herself enough for the guard to let her go then she sat down again. "Garrett, I'm begging you. You don't deserve this. If I'd been a better mother, a better person, none of this would have ever happened."

"Mom, I can't-"

"Just destroy the tape. It's over, baby. My sentence is up. I'm getting out soon. It's over. Let it go."

I had done all I could to take care of my sister. I think I did pretty well, too. She was a senior in high school, making excellent grades and she'd just been awarded a scholarship to Georgetown University. She wanted to attend the same school as Maddie. We'd finally gotten the happy lives we'd searched for. But I could no longer be happy knowing what I knew.

I wouldn't be able to see her graduate from high school or help her move into the freshman dorms, but as I drove to the police station with the tape in hand, I hoped Eden would always know how much I loved her.

# About the Author

Leslie DuBois lives in Charleston, South Carolina with her husband and two children. She currently attends the Medical University where she's earning her PhD in Biostatistics. Leslie enjoys writing stories and novels that integrate races. Her other novels include Guardian of Eden, The Queen Bee of Bridgeton and La Cienega Just Smiled coming November 2011. She also writes as Sybil Nelson. Visit her at www.LeslieDuBois.com to learn more.

Also from

Little Prince

Publishing

Kings

&

Queens

by

Courtney Vail

# CHAPTER 1
## Bad Plans

When the spindly finger of doom first poked Majesty five months ago, she'd shrugged it off with a "yeah, right," only to have her father end up near-headless in a ditch under a blanket of safety glass. These days, her shoulders stayed put. *Knew something would happen. Knew it!*     She clamped her jaw to quiet her stupid teeth. Should she whistle? Shout for help? Would it startle him or even be heard over the celebratory clamor by the diamond? Her teeth chattered and bones smarted as she searched every corner in her eyeshot for assistance and came up empty. Tension rolled down her back. She was his only hope. God help him.

Though his eye color remained a mystery, since he quivered on a ledge more than thirty feet above her and she was pretty sure she'd never more than glanced at him before, those windows to his soul bulged like half-dollars, minted with fear. Fear was *good*. That meant he didn't *want* to die, right?" At least not with a face-first plummet into blacktop.

Chilly wind swirled around her and whipped her chestnut locks into her face, yet she broke into a sweat and her limbs threatened to melt. She clutched her hair with fumbling fingers and shoved it into the back of her shirt as she sought a gem of inspiration.

What was his name even? *Crap!*

He, who was like three pounds heavier than the Crypt Keeper, and honestly not much cuter, shuffled his foot.

Gravel rained down and pricked Majesty's face, making her grimace and recoil. Knuckling sand out of her eye, she strained to extract his moniker from some dusty, mental file. His name...Nothing!

This guy seriously melted into the walls, which was probably why he wanted a splattery exeunt. But, he appeared to be second-guessing his death wish, clinging to the backside of Cedar Creek High, fingers spread wide like the blue ones on a strawberry poison dart frog.

Fetching the war slicker from her office off the gym should've been a speedy task, but this circus-act-gone-wrong had snagged her. Of course his life depended on her, a hot mess of seventeen who'd warn out more running shoes in recent time than birthday candles. Her, rather than someone who could think under duress without rattling off the gobs of fixings in various pints of Ben & Jerry's.

Majesty raised her plastic sleeve and glanced at her just-watch, which would've been a gadgety Garmin had she not gotten trumped last minute on eBay. "Well, jump already. What are ya waitin' for? Haven't got all day. Hear the frenzy? I've got a winners' battle to attend to, managerial duties to punch out, you know, the usual, 'cause we're rockin' a glorious, undefeated season."

"What? You think I should jump?"

"What do I know. Call a hotline. I can barely handle my

own turmoil, never mind yours. Unless you're holding a bat or glove, can't help ya, sorry. Crisis aversion is not in my job descrip." She leaned back on one leg and tucked her hands into her pockets, in case he could spot the severe tremor, then planted her other foot strong to keep it from tapping in time to the frantic pulse. Hopefully she wasn't playing this hand of Death all wrong. "What do you got to live for anyway?"

"Nothing. I'm so...tired."

"Take naps then. Less permanent."

"I mean...of having no friends."

"I thought you did. That Prince of Darkness guy? Warren Niles?"

"Yeah. One friend. Lucky me. As good as none."

"Oh, please. If you hate your situation, stop playing SimSuicide and change it. Find something you're good at. Make friends outside of school. I hear cults are very welcoming." "Every day is such a nightmare. You have no idea."

"Oh really? Do *you* wake up nearly every night, heaving from bloody dreams? Is *your* gut promising destruction like some crazy street guy forecasting the Apocalypse? Did *you* slam a door in your dad's face hours before he died? Does everyone you know, cops included, think you're a pestering loon 'cause "accident" doesn't sit right with you, nor the many things that are way off, like the car that keeps showing up on your street, with someone sitting in it, doing like, nothing? No? Oh no? Didn't think so. Life sucks for everyone. Jump or deal with it."

He held a moment of silence, hopefully, reconsidering the alternative to having gravel embedded in his brain. "You really slammed the door in your dad's face? On *that* day?"

Majesty closed her eyes and took deep breaths, then supplanted the barbed truth with something regarding the weather. *Yes*, she nodded, it was quite windy. The frickin' clattering leaves on roller coasters of gnarled branches proved it, as did Mikey's three-run, walk-off homer that had not-so-magically drifted a little more to the right.

"Man," he said. "So, even your best friends, Alec and Derek, think you're nuts?" Majesty winced that he knew exactly who her best friends were, while she couldn't even recall his stinkin' name. Surely she'd heard it at some point. She scratched her cheek. All she could come up with was Wheels, but that couldn't be right. She reopened her eyes and looked back at up at his vibrating knees.

"Yep. BFFs can break your heart too."

"Must suck to be you, oh, Queen of Misery."

"Most days."

He edged along the thin lip, and her heart leaped into her throat. She slapped her chest with splayed fingers.

His toes hung over, body swayed.

Despite her best effort to play cool cat, her shrill shriek as he wavered to catch balance throttled that guise to death.

"No! Don't!" She held her breath until he regained equilibrium.

He stayed there for several seconds, then ducked in through an open window. Majesty pumped her fist and let out a whoop. Well, at least her disastrous life was good for something. Maybe, comparatively, his seemed a net of butterflies. Likely was. Death was one nasty S.O.B., leaving her with a mountain of regret and an untouchable grief.

Smiling at her success and not paying attention, she spun right into someone and wobbled, stepping back. *Oh gothic lord.* "What do *you* want?" Aside from seldom hellos, she couldn't recall speaking to Warren before and wished to retract her crisp words.

"Let me guess. Jase?"

"Jase? Oh. Jaaase. Jason Wheeeeeler. Yep. He's safely off the brink." Her gaze pinballed from his dark lips to his crown of gelled daggers to his demon garb. She ground her teeth to stuff the bragging words dancing on her tongue, as his lack of shock and narrowed eyelids insisted he could more than one-up her.

"For now. Gotta lock that whackjob up some days. Your victory annihilation is about to commence," he said brusquely, his eyes spilling layers and layers of aches.

She cleared the sting from her throat. "Yeah. Thanks."

Before she could say anything closer to kind, he scuffled away, hands in pockets. *So weird.* Majesty hustled over to her gang of conquering Colts. From the trunk of weaponry remnants, she selected the best looking gun, though cracked and paltry. *Oh well. I never lose.*

Arm-shoved from behind, she jumped and spun to find Derek's light blue gems darkened in a glare. "Jerk," she said. "Looking to die faster?"

"Took you the hell long enough."

"Just saving another neck. My bad."

Gun in his fist, he punched his palm. "Come on, let's go. I'm It."

"The *Shit's* more like it," Alec said walking up to them, then laughed at himself. "Had to make him wait for ya."

Derek clenched the red stain on his shirt. "Only scored 'cause I wasn't looking, loser. You're *all* goin' down. I'm calling it now. The first total wipeout ever."

"Yeah. Still gotta get *me*." Majesty swept her finger over the red goop on Derek's shirt and sniffed it. "Wow. This looks and smells so real."

"Right. Goat's blood usually does," Alec said flatly, though the jest in his eyes gave him away. No doubt they'd chosen blood ammo for her anticipated reaction alone. But her dreams were no joke. They just didn't get it. She'd give 'em nothing though. Not even a blanch.

"Ooo, it's real? Delicious." Majesty slid her tainted

243

finger onto her tongue, closed her lips around it, then pulled it out clean with an erotic moan. "Mmm." It *was* real! *Nasty!*

But her nausea was well worth it, as their hilarity cut cold, faces scrunched into the sweetest sneers–Alec's taking the cake, with an Elvis snarl and all that glee dissolving in his eyes. "Epic fail trying to sickify me. Watch out. I fight hard and dirty."

"Alec'll fight ya. Dirty or not. Betcha you could take him down in three seconds."

"Mmm hmm. Poor thing. I'll be gentle."

"No way, baby," Alec whispered in her ear. "I like it rough." He left a kiss on her temple. "Good to know." She winked at him.

They waved her off and dashed for the thicket.

She tested her ammo, squirting her hand, gawking at the streaming ribbons of red. *Blood for everyone? It's fine. Don't be such a baby.*

Considering the capacity of these adjustable-nozzle super soakers, she didn't even want to think about how many buckets they'd bought or where or how? Though she had to admit this sort of upped the coolness of splatter hide and seek, she couldn't let 'em off the hook. *Just need a plan. Has to be good. Unforgettable. No, legendary.*

As she drew closer to the rowdy warriors, she whistled through her fingers to get the party started. What an impressive cry of the wolf! Her loudest ever. She lifted a soaring whoop again, but it fell far short of the first's magnificence.

Movement caught her eye by the fence, and she shivered and stopped cold. *What the heck's he still doing here?* Warren glared from behind the chain links like he could slay her beloved Colts with his virulence alone. Maybe he could. Maybe that's why her chills wouldn't die.

244

\* \* \* \*

Finished with player updates, an article for the team site and most deliciously, the *call*, Majesty laughed, dropping her office phone into its cradle. Getting to gloat to the Wasps' Athletic Director thrilled as a definite managerial perk. The Colts and Wasps usually faced off in the regionals, but the Dragons just scorched the lousy buzzers, 12-5.

But, every ounce of funny was suddenly slain by the unrelenting sting from nearly being taken out by Derek. Cornered in the brush, the last one standing, and "Time's up!" was what had saved her? *Disgraceful.* Majesty groaned, tucking her hair under her cap, then snatched flavored water from her mini-fridge and kissed school goodbye.

She took off running unhurried, but if she wanted to punch it, her 5'3" stature didn't hinder her speed. She was primed from racing and keeping pace with her pack.

She darted around to the front and down the driveway and turned left toward the center of Cedar Creek and away from the homes with yippy purse dogs and diamond-studded mailboxes.    The sprinkle of storefronts, a second-run cinema, St. Mark's, one restaurant, one gas station and Spanky's–a mini-golf/ice cream shop-gone-wild–desperately needed more company.

Utility pole banners still up from the St. Paddy's Day parade enticed her to search for surprise additions amongst bunnies and flowers. *No screwing dogs or beheaded rats yet? Boring, people. Get with it.* These sugary spring-things always flapped in the wind beside mini American flags until the day after the Independence Day fireworks…which was not necessarily on the 4th…or even in July. She'd have to be on the lookout for the perfect demented treasure to tack up

245

before then. Little sound was lovelier than a chorus of old lady shrieks and tsks.

After passing Fisher Price village and the lions guarding Markie's cathedral, she booked it into the common, a fancy name for an ill-equipped park. Woods laced through town, but this particular strip aroused whispers. Three kids, holding hands and singing *Ring around the Rosie*, stopped and gawked.

One cried, "She's goin' in. Must not be ascared a the spooks."

Traversing from grass for dirt, Majesty chuckled that Alec's tale about the wood-dwelling people-creatures endured. "They grow more fierce each day, waiting for their kings and queens to come and lead them to overtake the area, the country and eventually, the world."

Six years ago, a girl disappeared. Theories abounded, but most of the children believed, "The spooks got her."

Crows griped about the invasion and the drooping sun spilled beams through the evergreen towers, creating an inky leviathan war deep in the thick. Majesty growled as anxiety resurged. Near the tripod, where three towns converged, and a coven reportedly danced nude, she slowed to a stroll. Birds departed the treetops in a flurry of flapping wings, but one crow remained, voicing stern warnings to friends...or maybe her. She gulped her drink, enjoying its grape hint. When glitchy male voices found her ears, she froze with a bead of water dripping from her mouth.

"So, everything's set?"

"Yep. Got the guns, supplies. It's a go."

Majesty searched. *There...little over ten yards.*

"Hope...doesn't blow up in our faces. Thought we were gonna kill one. Those people won't know what hit 'em."

*People?...Can't see anything!* Imaginary ants tingled her neck and her legs wobbled with each step she took toward a concealing tree. She braced herself and peered around the trunk. Fatigues, bulky vests and face-engulfing Buffs, muffled and muddled all identifiers. *Great!* "That's the beauty...They'll learn how dead and buried their Jesus is when...doesn't help...start shooting up the church. Haven't...how many I wanna off yet. Needs to be impressive...national coverage. Let's snatch our gear...do this lame paintball thing, get back to our real deal."

They headed for the even deader town of Megan's Corner. *No. Wait!* Majesty leaned forward, shifting her weight. *If I could just...*A stick snapped underfoot. The taller one stopped and whacked his buddy's arm. She cringed and jerked back.

"Shh...Hear somethin'?" They were likely debating the noise she'd stupidly made in the whispers she couldn't make out, but the clatter of them moving through the woodland was deafening.

Sweat dripped from Majesty's temples and frightened fairies fluttered beneath her skin. She stood motionless as the rustling drew much too close. Shoved into flight, she took off like a sprinter at the shot. Water sloshed on her leg, awakening goose bumps with its chill. She chucked the bottle and cap into reaching shrubs.

Muddled threats nipped at her heels, but agility and swiftness aided her evasion, as well as knowing the woods, not well, but well enough.

Majesty bolted through the clearing, rounded a bend and deserted the path. Busting through brushwood as fast as she could, she spotted a hollow. She jumped into its bowl of dead foliage with way too much crunch, slid under a bush and clammed her mouth with her hands to prevent gasping. She swallowed to rid the tightness that was crawling up her throat.

"Some girl. See anything?"

247

"No."

She tried to catch vocal distinctions, already smothered by a babbling stream. She swept a tickling spider off her arm, lifting freakin' trumpet blasts into the air. *Idiot!* Her heartbeat drummed in her ears as she muscled her gaze through branches.

"Gone."

The watery white noise had proven a godsend for her foolish misstep and cranky stomach, now bellowing for food.

One of them kicked debris her way and a fleck of something hit her eye. She closed her aching eye and covered it with her fingers.

After a string of salty slurs, one said, "Hair was hidden...Colts shirt." "Good. One of our own. Should...find her."

She shuddered. Agony seduced her to dislodge the foreign body with her knuckle. She couldn't wait. "But what if she—"

"No one can stop us, especially some girl. We're in control. I'll find her first...eradicate her." Their nerve-grating footfalls walked away, veering into silence.

Majesty finally allowed her lungs to yank air.

She'd never been so petrified...except for the time men in blue had come to her door...and she just *knew*.

*Summer 2011*
*Little Prince Publishing*

www.ingramcontent.com/pod-product-compliance
Lightning Source LLC
Chambersburg PA
CBHW022005170626
46808CB00001B/289